SHOOTOUT CITY . . .

Suddenly, the street was silent.

Then a man stepped out into the street.

"Slocum!" His hard voice rang like a bullet down the stony street, waiting, and some people who spoke of it afterwards thought they heard its echo.

"I am right here," John Slocum said as he turned and faced the big man with the two tied-down six guns.

"I been waiting for you, Slocum. You sonofabitch."

They faced each other now in a silence that nobody could ever have measured.

Until at last it was broken.

"I've been waiting for you, too, you *dead* sonofabitch!" And John Slocum drew and everybody heard the crack of the bullet from the .44 Colt, but nobody could remember later what they really saw . . .

This book also contains a preview
of Giles Tippette's
exciting new western novel
Cherokee.

JAKE LOGAN

FINAL DRAW

BERKLEY BOOKS, NEW YORK

FINAL DRAW

A Berkley Book / published by arrangement with
the author

PRINTING HISTORY
Berkley edition / June 1993

ISBN: 0-425-13707-4

A BERKLEY BOOK ® TM 757,375
Berkley Books are published by The Berkley Publishing Group,
200 Madison Avenue, New York, New York 10016.
The name "BERKLEY" and the "B" logo
are trademarks belonging to Berkley Publishing Corporation.

PRINTED IN THE UNITED STATES OF AMERICA

10 9 8 7 6 5 4 3 2 1

FINAL DRAW

1

There were some people living in Finality Gulch who claimed the town to be the best part of hell. Then there were others who allowed as how it was the worst. But John Slocum was keeping an open mind on the subject. He had ridden into the mountain town only that morning, and what the population thought of their toehold on the frontier was no concern of his. He was here for a purpose, and the sooner he got shut of his business the sooner he'd be free to ride where he'd wanted to head for in the first place. The Sweetwater country.

He was a big man under that black Stetson hat, broad-shouldered as a boxcar, lean-hipped, lithe, and a man could sometimes find granite in the handsome face, sometimes humor. In his thirties or thereabouts, he had big hands, the kind that knew exactly what was required of them—be it rope, rein, gun, fistfight, or, as a number of women would have attested, other adventures.

Some people figured him for part Indian. He carried that look, that grace of movement; a relaxed alertness like an animal. He looked like a man who could handle pain.

It had never mattered to John Slocum what people thought of him. He had himself, and that was all he needed. It was all any man needed; the way of a man who lived free and was aiming to stay that way.

He had just now stepped out of the Generosity Saloon into the late morning sunlight. At that exact moment, a young boy came running down the street and almost knocked into him, swerving just in time. Slocum had been taking his tobacco pouch out of the pocket of his hickory shirt to build himself a smoke when the boy so narrowly averted a collision.

The big man shifted his weight as the boy sped on, not spilling even a grain of tobacco. He watched the figure grow smaller as it crossed the railroad tracks and disappeared into the Cabbage Patch, that section of every western town which held the stock pens, the hangouts for trail drivers, the saloons and dancehalls, and of course the wild girls.

Standing easy, Slocum finished building his smoke, ran the edge of the thin paper along his tongue and twisted the end of the cigarette, finishing the entire movement as though it were a dance, with the white tube ending up between his lips. Without breaking the rhythm, he struck the head of a lucifer one-handed with his thumbnail, and cupping the flame—still with only the one hand—lighted up.

He was standing in the shade of Gildersleeve's General Store and taking up just about all of it. He still tasted some of the dust from the long trail north and west out of Laramie, even though he'd lowered a big mug of beer in the Generosity Saloon and Dancing Establishment. He took another drag on his smoke, then held it between thumb and forefinger, sheltering it in his palm, one-handed—he'd always believed in economy of movement—and spat at the hitching post in front of him, hitting it plumb center.

He was thinking of the old sourdough at the bar in the Generosity who claimed that "By God, the Gulch is gonna one day bust hell outta the country one way or t'other an' more sooner than later an' that's a gut!"

The rickety old boy had said it when he and some other rheumy-eyed veterans of the bottle had been supporting the long mahogany while Slocum listened, hoping to get a line on the town. He'd been standing nearby, easy but not too close to the bar in case of sudden action. He'd learned it early; if a man wanted to live to see tomorrow then he'd damn well better be awake today.

Right now, viewing the town from the boardwalk just outside the Generosity, he had no doubts about the difficulty of his task, nor any illusions about the man who had pinned it on him: Heavy Hank Finnegan. He remembered their confrontation just a few days before . . .

"I want you to find him. I want you to find Otis—dead or alive! You figure out how!" Finnegan's eyes were hard as stone as he said those words.

"I heard you the first ten times you said it," Slocum replied drily. "Tell me one more time and I'll more'n likely forget it."

They were in the marshal's office in Ten Town, and Slocum was feeling more than a little anger in Finnegan. Heavy Hank Finnegan was trouble for sure. Short on brains, he made up for it with cunning. Slocum knew the man to be a "ruthless sonofabitch", the phrase used of him throughout the saloons and Cabbage Patches of the Wyoming Territory.

"You won't forget," Finnegan snapped back at him. " 'Specially don't forget why it is you're working for the law!"

Slocum brought his hard eyes right on the man in the wooden armchair, taking in the big iron jaw, the bull neck, the wide chest, and hands like hams.

"Finnegan, I am not working for the law and especially not for the likes of yourself. You got that? I mean it!"

Finnegan's eyes glittered. Slocum held them until they blinked. Then Finnegan looked away, just for a second. His eyes whipped back almost instantly, but Slocum had made his point.

Finnegan sniffed, cleared his nose, hawked, and spat into the brass cuspidor beside the desk.

"My deputies picked you up, Slocum. On my orders. Masters and Hendry Pills brought you in. Charged with switching brands. That spells rustling in this man's country, mister. Shit, man, I could have you necktied!" And then suddenly without warning, "Just who the fuckin' hell do you think you are!" He roared the words, his eyes almost popping all the way out of his huge head, his purple face bursting with rage. But right on cue a fit of coughing overtook him and he collapsed back into his chair—having half risen in his anger—and began to choke.

Slocum sat calmly watching him.

"Finnegan," he said quietly. "I am no bounty hunter. You get someone else to do your dirty work. You haven't got a damn thing on me except what you've cooked up. So don't push!"

Finnegan was still purple in the face as he tried to stop coughing. In another moment, the lawman regained control of himself.

"You'll do what I tell you, Slocum. God damn you! Think you're King Shit, you do. You'll do what I say, however, on account of I know about that little problem with you and Miller and his stock. By God I can read a running iron with the best of 'em. And I know damn well, same as any cattleman would, just who them calves Miller's got up there would mother up to if let be!"

Slocum had turned halfway in his chair to take his cigarette off his lip with his thumb and middle finger and drop it easily into one of the cuspidors near him. Now he turned his full attention again on the lawman seated in front of him, instantly noticing the smirk that was just starting across that big, red face.

"Finnegan . . ." Slocum, leaning back in his chair, said the name softly, sounding like a caution to a child. "You know same as me that them cows I was bunching on the south fork were rebranded with a running iron, and you know too that a whole hell-uva lot more than likely it was the Seaver men who done it. And you know damn well that I was returning those beeves to their rightful owner. To John Miller, a friend of mine who was stove up and couldn't sit a saddle this good while. Stove up, mind you, on account of the beating he got from some of the Seaver fellers."

Even before Slocum had finished Heavy Hank was shaking his head like a feisty bull. His words came out harshly. "And you know, by God, mister, that Wells, Fargo's got a likely notion that you be working for Morgan Marks, not only rustling beef but stepping right on Wells, Fargo's toes by holding up the Casper Limited. That is two crimes on you—cattle rustling *and* armed robbery." He leaned all the way back in his chair now. "That's it. Now I told 'em I knew you when they sent two men down to Ten Town inquirin'. I told 'em I didn't know you well, but I told them I didn't believe you did the train. I said to them may-be the cattle, but I said a definite 'no' to the train holdup. I personally know that ain't your style." He sniffed, keeping his eyes on Slocum. " 'Course they do know you sided with Nate Champion in the Wyoming Stockgrowers trouble."

"Wells, Fargo had nothing to do with that shebang," Slocum said, coming down hard on the words. "And you know that."

"I'd say they'd be interested in it, Mr. Slocum. On account of they're interested in yourself."

"They don't know me." But Slocum already could hear the answer to that.

"They do now," said Heavy Finnegan. "They for sure do now." And the grin was wide on his big face.

"I've got a lot to thank you for," Slocum said drily.

"You will when you locate Otis for me." The grin was wide. "Otherwise, well . . . well, let's not let there be any otherwise about it. You find Otis for me. I mean that, like I first told you. I don't want you to do anything with him. Just locate him. And I want to know what he's doing up around Finality."

He sniffed. "Then, since you're actin' like my deputy, Wells, Fargo might see their way clear to droppin' any charges against you an' Miller."

"How long has Otis been out of Laramie?"

"Ten days—give or take."

"And you say he's headed north?"

"He is headed for Finality Gulch, and environs. His old stamping ground."

"How do you know that? You sure?"

Heavy Hank looked at him carefully then, as though deciding whether to say any more. He sniffed, then scratched his crotch. He said, "Where would you be headed if you knew where you'd cached yer takin's from all them robberies?"

Slocum was silent to that. And he knew that the two of them were thinking the same thing. That Otis would have more than a few people asking the same question.

"Likely to run into somethin' like a crowd then," Slocum observed.

"Reckon." Heavy Hank's big head bobbed slowly in assent.

"You'll stick to your word on John Miller then. You'll lay off him, and his boy."

"Huh."

"You'll call off Wells, Fargo. Sure I rode with Miller, but we never held up any trains or stagecoaches, or anything for that matter. And you by God know that. The real trouble is he's got prime land right up on the North Fork of the Greybull. And him and his son Tommy always kept their noses clean." He stood then, facing the man in the deep chair. "You keep your nose clean, Finnegan, and we'll get along fine." He pushed his tongue into his cheek, making a little ball as he held his eyes firmly on the lawman.

A silence moved into the room now as the tableau continued without either man making a move.

At last Finnegan spoke. "Reckon you know Otis rode with some real fast company in the old days."

"Reckon I do."

" 'Course, he spent all that time in prison. You don't get any younger in a place like Laramie." Heavy Hank Finnegan shifted in his chair. "How many years was it? A dozen?"

"I'd reckon a good dozen," Slocum said, knowing very well that Finnegan knew exactly how long Otis had been in the penitentiary.

"I do believe his gang—all of them . . . well, I heard they cashed in or just up and disappeared."

"Maybe you can figger Otis is the last of the bunch. 'Leastways that's what everybody seems to figure."

"The law sure does," Finnegan said, nodding his big head in agreement.

An even heavier silence invaded the room then. After

a while as the light at the windowsill grew darker, Finnegan spoke.

"He must've been a real sonofabitch, 'least that's what I hear . . . I mean like how he double-crossed Whistler."

"In that business that's the way you get ahead," Slocum said. "Where you been all your life, Finnegan?"

They both chuckled at that, loosening the moment appreciably.

"They say Jake Whistler was the fastest gun ever. I mean *ever*!" Heavy Hank raised himself a little out of the depths of his armchair in appreciation of what he had just said.

"Don't look like he was fast enough for Otis, I'd say." Slocum cocked an eye at Heavy Hank then.

"Otis shot him in the back," Hank Finnegan said.

Slocum, looking into the middle distance, nodded. "That's just what I said. Otis was faster."

2

Indeed it looked like maybe a dry-gulching for himself some days later—yesterday, as a matter of fact—when he rode the Appaloosa up the long draw not far east of Finality Gulch. He drew rein and sat there in his high-cantled stock saddle, looking down at the dead man, while knowing clear as a chunk of ice on his back that he was not alone.

Even before the voice came out of the small stand of cottonwoods he knew he had company. And too, it hadn't really been all that much of a surprise. Even before he'd read the way the Appaloosa cocked his ears he'd spotted the hoofprints. Not far from the stand of fir and pine. He was already reading the tracks of two horses, one being led, as he gentled the Appaloosa, who sure wasn't happy about that dead man lying right there in full view at the side of the narrow trail.

Slocum's hands moved very slowly, keeping close to his body as he called out, "I'm reaching for my makings, mister, so don't get yerself in an uproar. I am not a lawman and I never saw this man before—dead or alive."

In the silence that held the tense tableau he drew his

sack of Bull Durham and his papers from the pocket of his hickory shirt and began building himself a smoke.

The voice from the cottonwoods was grainy, but firm with authority, backed for sure by weaponry. It had simply ordered him to stay where he was.

Now it said, "What you doin' up on Barley Creek?"

Slocum allowed a beat . . . and another.

"I got you right in my sights, mister, and I ain't gonna ask you again."

This piece of information however had furnished Slocum with what he wanted to know; the more exact location of the gunman.

"I am minding my own business, mister," he said. "And what are you doing throwing down on me?"

And he was out of the saddle, drawing the Colt .44 and aiming three shots into the trees where he'd caught not only the man's sound but the slight movement of leaves only a second before.

There was a yelp of pain, followed by cursing and a rifle shot whining aimlessly into the big sky.

"I got you in *my* sights," Slocum snapped. "Come on out, slow. Or the next one won't just nick you."

"I be comin'. Just hold it. Don't throw down on me!" These words were followed by some brisk cursing as Slocum heard his target moving through the brush.

"I can still see you, mister. Come out slow, and throw the Henry out here ahead of you."

"Knowed it was a Henry, huh? Got good ears, ain't you?"

"Maybe that's how come I lived this long," Slocum said drily.

And now the figure appeared as the rifle came sailing out of his hideout.

"Didn't expect to be goin' up against Wild Bill hisself in person fer Chrissakes!"

"You're not," Slocum said, and there was no funning in his voice as he stood there. "You're up against Slocum."

"Never heard of you, mister."

"You have now," Slocum said, grating each word.

He had a good view now of his would-be assailant. The man standing before him was almost totally hidden behind the wildest stand of gray whiskers Slocum had ever seen. The wiry hair was charging in every direction. Judging by the way the man moved, Slocum figured him for more than sixty-some. One hand was like a claw, the rusty-looking fingers bent back on themselves; his bony shoulders pushing up like hooks through an ancient shirt. His nose looked broken, with a drop of water hanging from its end and his eyes were rheumy, while his jaws kept working at his chewing tobacco like a prairie dog worrying a choice morsel.

Suddenly all those whiskers began to move faster and he let fly at a nearby clump of sage.

"I be alone."

"Excepting for myself," Slocum said, his words cold.

The old-timer cocked his head, his milky eyes widening in surprise. "How did you figger out I didn't have a backup?"

"I figured anyone making as much noise as yourself wouldn't be likely to have anybody else wanting to be around him at such a time."

"Shit! Shit take it!" He yanked off his battered black hat and threw it on the ground. "An' I was tryin' my damndest best to be real silent like so's you wouldn't even know I was there, by God." The iron-gray head wagged, and he reached up and scratched just above his right ear. "I keep tryin' to be as quiet as a damn Sioux an' all, but it's a real jasper it is. Damn it all, I'm gettin' old!"

But Slocum wasn't going with any chitchat. "Got any

more hardware there?" His tone was flat as a milled board, but demanded a quick answer.

"Nope. And I be alone."

"We already settled that." Slocum nodded toward the dead man. "Friend of yourn'?"

Something that looked like a painful grin appeared around all those whiskers. "Not no more, even if he was, but he wasn't."

Slocum slowly let the hammer down on his cocked handgun and slipped the weapon back into its holster. "So who sent you to dry-gulch me?"

"Nobody. I be riding fence for my own outfit, the Double C. Figgered you fer one of Rhine's men. But now I see otherwise."

"Who is Rhine?"

"You ain't heard of Rhine? You dunno Rhine?" The heavy eyebrows shot up toward the corrugated forehead and the yellow eyes rimmed with red bulged in amazement.

Slocum said nothing.

"I see you be a man of few words," his prisoner said, and his tone was careful.

Slocum spat at a clump of loose sage near his feet. "And I use them few now and again," he said.

"Rhine is the big man in this country. Bark Rhine." His eyes swept the horizon behind Slocum.

He reached carefully for his chewing tobacco, and brought out his clasp knife. With his good right hand he cut off a generous slice and slipped it into his mouth, the wicked-looking blade sparkling under sunlight.

"A stockgrower—huh," said Slocum, squinting at the other man.

"That's the size of it—plus a few other things."

"You're saying he owns."

"Like about everythin' this side of hell."

"He owns yourself?" Slocum asked suddenly, cock-ing his head just a little to one side, his eyes directly on the old man.

"He'd like to, I reckon." He wagged his head. "Mister, there ain't a whole helluva lot to own on a man seventy-two an' a half goin' on seventy-five." And then he added, "An' with a shot-up hand to boot."

"Maybe," Slocum allowed slowly. "Maybe. But, you're working for Rhine now, ain't you?"

"Like now and again."

"I am askin' if you are right now!" Slocum snapped out the words, his eyes boring into the old man.

The nod was slow, but it was clear.

"You know Ridey Bones?" Slocum asked. "His outfit's supposed to be up here between Pitchfork and Stud Wells. Thereabouts. You know him?"

The old man was shaking his head. "Don't know Bones personally, but his outfit's yonder. Under side of them rimrocks." And he nodded toward Slocum's left. "High up. Don't know Bones. Exceptin' I have heard he is no man to mess with." He nodded toward the corpse. "Somebody shot him. It wasn't me."

"Even Rhine?" And Slocum was staring directly at the other man. "Rhine doesn't mess with him? With Bones?"

Slocum watched the old man's eyes widen, really large. But he didn't answer.

"What is your name?" Slocum asked, as a sudden thought hit him.

"Slattery."

"Thought it might be Bones." He was looking hard at the old man, still not sure where the feeling he had came from. There was something out of line, but he couldn't name it.

"I ain't Bones," the old man said. "And by God, for the matter of that I sure as hell wouldn't want to be right now."

"Why not?" Slocum said, and his question was a demand.

"On account of Otis."

"Otis . . ."

"Maybe a bit before your time."

"Otis—he was in with Jake Whistler, I do believe," Slocum said.

Something had been worrying at Slocum ever since he'd asked about Ridey Bones. "You sure you don't work for Bones?" he asked now.

And he saw the flush come into the other man's face, under those whiskers. "I just told you, I work for Rhine."

"I know you did."

"Then why'd you ask about Bones, fer Chrissakes!"

"Thought you might change your mind," Slocum said, and his voice was cool.

"Jesus . . . !"

Slocum grinned then, a cold grin. " 'Pears to me that if that's Bones's spread up yonder, and across that creek there is Rhine's, then Mr. Rhine's got to be feeling some kind of interest in this part of the country, and so you and maybe those other two riders I seen while we've been gabbing are like protecting Bones's outfit. The way I see it, that figgers pretty plain."

"Could be that way."

And again Slocum was swept by the feeling of something off that had hit him earlier. "I am saying that Rhine is protecting Bones's outfit but not for Bones. At least that is what it looks like."

The old man suddenly pursed his lips together hard. "You're meaning . . . ?"

"I am meaning just what I am saying." Slocum's words came out firmly and stood between the two of them. And Slocum just let them stay there.

Finally the old man spoke. "You're saying—it 'pears

to me—that Bones is . . ."

But Slocum cut right in, his words falling between them like a top poker hand. "I am saying, mister, it's plain as a whiffle tree that you are Ridey Bones."

He watched the other man's brow tighten.

"What you want with me, mister." The words were said more as statement than question.

Instead of answering, Slocum let his attention swing toward the rimrocks where the old man had told him Ridey Bones had his spread.

"Mister," he said, bringing his eyes back to the man standing in front of him. "I want you to tell me where I can find Otis."

3

It had been a wild shot; figuring the old buzzard who'd said his name was Slattery for actually being Ridey Bones himself—in person.

It was clear right off that Bones was damn reluctant to talk. But Slocum saw that his guess had paid off. The man was definitely rattled.

At the same time, he swiftly saw that Ridey Bones was no simpleton, and by no means a man to be gulled into going against himself.

"You got time we'll head back to the outfit," The old man said after ruminating a minute or two.

Slocum nodded. "Just remember I'll be watching you real close."

"Mister, I ain't no dumbbell. I seen how you handle that .44. And as a matter of fact I do believe I have heard something about you." He spat suddenly, swiftly, and with evident accuracy at a small lizard, almost flattening the poor animal in saliva and tobacco.

Slocum said nothing to these revelations, missing nothing as he read the horizon, the rim of timber up ahead, the trail that they were following, and the trail behind them.

It wasn't far to the Double C spread, and they rode mostly in silence.

Bones told him that he had a couple of part-time hands, like himself getting on in years; the Double C only needing them for roundup and branding and such, like the spring gather when stock from one outfit would get mixed with another. And a man needed sharp eyes.

The outfit looked deserted when he rode in with Bones. They dismounted in the corral and Bones stripped his bay pony. Slocum, not knowing how long he would be staying, ground-hitched the Appaloosa.

"You kin throw yer duffel in the bunkhouse if you've a mind to," said the old man. And Slocum was surprised at his sudden offer, though it was clearly grudging. Until this moment he'd felt mostly suspicion and hostility. But evidently he had passed some kind of test during their ride to the ranch, which was tucked close under the rimrocks overlooking the long valley sweeping below them, all the way back down to Finality Gulch and beyond. Across the valley were more mountains, all of them snowcapped, mantled in white even though it was the beginning of summer.

Slocum favored the thin air. He'd always liked the mountains best, which was one of the main reasons he wanted to visit the Sweetwater, but that damned Finnegan had bungled that for him. At any rate for the time being.

"I'll rustle some Arbuckle," the old man said as he shut the corral gate behind their horses. "I got the missus here, but she got a game leg and she don't get about any too good."

"Could use some coffee," Slocum said agreeably.

It was a log house, as indeed were the other buildings—including the bunkhouse which Bones had indicated with a throw of his thumb, and a barn

next to the corral. Slocum noticed right away that
whoever had built the outfit knew his business. And
he noted too that the stock they'd come across on the
way in—both cattle and a couple of horses, who he'd
decided likely to be the old man's team—were in good
shape.

The surprise came as they approached the door of the
cabin and it was suddenly opened. But not by anyone
Slocum could have imagined as Bones's wife.

"This here's Janey," Bones said.

Slocum found himself almost with his mouth hanging open before he recovered himself sufficiently to
say an audible hello to the gorgeous creature standing
there before him.

"This here feller throwed down on me over at Barley Creek, lookin' like he could just as lief part my
hair with the way he was handling that handgun of
hisn'."

"Now Grandpa, maybe you could tell me the gentleman's name. I am not really interested in his ability to
handle a gun."

Slocum picked up on the tone of disapproval mixed
with good humor and a mollifying attitude toward her
grandfather. At the same time, he realized what was
going on inside himself after he had recovered from the
shock of meeting the dark-haired, brown-eyed beauty who appeared to be completely self-possessed and
wholly at ease with the unexpected company.

Her smile was delightful as she gave him a little nod,
and then indicated that he should follow her.

"Gram is lying down." she said, as she led the way
though the living room and into the kitchen.

Slocum could see peeled logs, solidly constructed
into a sound building, some rugs, and a neatness that
he didn't often find in homes that far from town.

"I am sure you'd like some coffee," the girl said as

she indicated a chair for the visitor.

"I would," Slocum said. "Thank you, Ma'am . . . Miss," he added quickly as his eye dropped to her ring finger, which was bare.

"Might I know your name, sir?" she asked.

"John Slocum."

"The feller throwed down on me," Bones said again, seemingly surprised that such a thing could have happened.

"Grandpa . . ." She looked at Slocum. "Grandpa sometimes forgets that he is close on seventy-five and not quite as spry as when he was twenty."

And Slocum found her smile delightful.

Indeed, he found everything about her unbelievably exciting.

Meanwhile, Bones didn't appear to notice anything. But Slocum could feel something coming from the girl. She couldn't have been more than twenty-three or four at the most, he decided. She was shy and self-possessed all at the same time, and now a flush suddenly appeared in her cheeks, as though she didn't know which way to go. Slocum decided she was marvelous, as he grinned at her.

"Janey's out here visiting," Bones said. "She been staying up in Pierre with Millie's folks, studying some stuff."

"I am studying anthropology, Grandpa," Janey said, and she smiled warmly at Slocum, and then stuck her tongue out at her grandparent.

But Slocum could see she was far from angry; he could tell it was a game they played. And he felt good. How different the old geezer seemed. Not at all like he'd been on the trail when he'd braced him with that Henry rifle.

This thought brought him back to the business at hand, and Heavy Hank Finnegan's demand that he find Otis. He took a breath then. For while the girl was real special he realized he had better keep his eye on business. Friendly though both Bones and his granddaughter were he had that feeling that he couldn't take anything for granted. And that this was no time to forget what he was doing up here in the Absaroka country in the first place.

He waited while they had coffee, talking a bit about the stock, the weather, the coming spring roundup. Then, catching the girl picking up on her grandfather's look and rising to her feet, he realized the moment had come for him to get down to business.

When the girl left the room, Slocum lifted his mug of coffee, drained it, and set it down on the table in front of him. He was about to speak when he heard the horses.

Bones, who had started to doze a little, the way old men sometimes do, heard them too and was suddenly wide awake. Slocum was already on his feet.

"Better let me handle it," the old man said.

"Sounds like three," Slocum said.

"Figgers." The nod was slight, but the old man was fully alert and on his feet. "Company . . . an' it for sure ain't social." He stepped swiftly across the kitchen to a closet.

"You got a goose gun?" Slocum asked.

"I do."

"You talk to them," Slocum said. "I'll cover you." He was peering from the side of the window. "They come like that in daylight," he said, making it a hard statement, though it was understood as a question.

Bones's tone was like wire. "They goddamn come when they goddamn well please."

The hoofbeats were louder now as the horsemen swept past the corral and pulled up in a sheet of dust right outside the door of the cabin. He saw the hard, red faces of the men in the fading light.

One of the horsemen called out.

"Bones!"

Ridey Bones had already started to open the door. And now he stood in the doorway with the shotgun ready, his rifle standing right inside, so the men on horseback couldn't see it. That way they couldn't be sure whether or not the old man had extra weapons or other backup; which was how Slocum had read it. That old man was sharp, he could see. And he wasn't afraid.

"What do you want?"

His tone was hard. Slocum, watching from the corner window at the side of the house away from the men, could see the riders, who were not dismounting. One of them in fact, was fighting his horse who'd spooked at something or other and was high-stepping about, lifting plenty of dust.

The three men had the look of hard riders, gunswifts; especially when he took into account their display of weaponry. Each carried a brace of handguns, and two were holding Winchesters.

Slocum noticed now that Bones was holding the sawed-off scatter-gun easy and not pointing it directly at his three visitors. He was standing there hard as stone; and Slocum—out of sight—had been able to feel the man's strength. He was also well aware that the sun was almost down to the horizon and dusk was falling. It would be dark soon enough to cover those gunmen, he was thinking, but they must have a reason why they'd picked this time of day for a visit. The visitors sat their horses like they were ready to drive them right through that log cabin.

But Slocum had his surprise when he heard Bones's voice. It wasn't any longer the voice of an old man maybe not so damn sure of himself, an old geezer who'd known better times. This was a man who reminded Slocum of something, or maybe it had been someone, he wasn't sure; but it was a man standing there with that scatter-gun ready to brace those three owlhooters.

"We got a message for Bones," said the man on the middle horse, a big bay with three white stockings. Slocum saw that the man was looking past Bones; at the cabin, then dropped his eyes to the barrel of the goose gun.

"Reckon that's you," the rider to his left said.

"Say yer piece and get yer ass off my range," Bones said, his voice as hard as the barrel of the gun he was holding.

Slocum saw the spokesman's hand tighten on the reins he'd been holding as he spat over his horse's withers. He was a wiry man and he needed a shave. Even through the dusk, Slocum knew the sneer was there on that lean face.

"There's an old friend of yours says he'll meet you in town, Bones."

"Whoever that be you can tell him I'm right here. If he's got the guts for a face-to-face and not a dry-gulchin'."

Slocum was again surprised to hear such a strong tone coming from Ridey Bones.

"Tomorrer mornin' 'round about noontime," said the thin man on the dappled pony. "Reckon you better bring yer popgun along with you."

"You tell that sonofabitch I'll be right here. Now git! I mean right now! I don't 'preciate your kind of scum round my place!"

"Tomorrow at Finality, the forenoon," said the man on the dappled pony. And there was laughter all over his big red face.

"Git!" Bones spat the word like a nail.

For a brief moment the three waited, then the dappled pony and steeldust horse started to act feisty, both fighting the bit.

Slocum could sure tell that those three hadn't liked that old man ordering them. Then the one on the big bay who had first spoken wheeled his horse. And the other two right away followed him.

Back in the house, seated at the kitchen table, Slocum waited until the girl was out of the room. Now he could hear her talking with her grandmother in the bedroom, where she had gone to see if there was anything needed.

"What you got?" Bones suddenly asked. "You don't appear too all-fired happy about them proceedings."

"Are you?"

The old man didn't answer. Instead he cleared his nose with a loud hawking, then let fly at the coal scuttle. His aim was true, but at that instant Janey walked in, her face tight with horror.

"Grandpa, you know how that spitting in the coal bucket upsets Grandma; I do wish you wouldn't do it!"

"Better out and bear the shame than hold it in an' bear the pain," her grandfather intoned in a sepulchral voice.

But then seeing that his granddaughter was truly upset, he held up a mollifying hand, saying, "I won't do it again. I promise."

"You've got a whole lot of acreage out there on which you can spit, Grandfather, dear, so why keep it indoors?"

"Got a point there, girl. Why deny the country the benefit of some extra water. By golly, the way things have been goin' of late, it might be this good while 'fore we get some relievin' rain." And he dropped a slow wink at Slocum.

Slocum then heard the door of the bedroom close and the dim sound of the women talking was cut off. He was grateful for the privacy.

"You look like you got somethin' to say," Ridey Bones said, squinting at Slocum. "I can tell you're suspicioning somethin'."

"I want to go out and take a look."

"Good enough. You want cover?"

"Might be a good move, but keep out of sight." He rose to his feet, and now Bones followed suit.

Slocum walked to the kitchen door.

"I'll cover you from the window here," Bones said, "Depending on which way you're going."

"I want to study those prints."

"There'll be three sets, besides my bay and your Appaloosa."

"I got an idea there might be another set."

The old man's forehead rose in a series of wrinkles. "Meanin'?"

"Meaning, four rode in but only three rode out."

Bones's eyes whipped to the window from which a corner of the barn and a bit of the corral could be seen. "I see you eyeing that direction," he said, and he was chewing faster now. "You reckon we got a visitor, that it?"

"I had a feeling I heard another horse comin' in, whilst you were jawing with the three. Now, they rode in from that side yonder that's blind to anybody in the house here. And also it was beginning to get dark, like twilight and that kind of light now and again can be harder to see something in than when it's full dark."

Ridey was nodding. "That's what I know," he said. He sniffed, and chewing rapidly, paused for just the time required to spit, once again into the coal bucket. "Shit take it," he muttered. "Forgot."

"They could have got someone in the barn is what I'm sayin'."

"With me figurin' it was all going to be at high noon tomorrer in town. The sonofabitches! It's an old trick."

"It'll be dark pretty quick," Slocum observed. "He drew his six gun and checked it, then dropped it back into its holster.

"You'd best wait till dark then," the old man said. "Exceptin' it better be me goes and checks it out and not yourself."

"If I go out now he won't do anything," Slocum said. "Not in this light. And also, him seeing me about like that he'll figure we don't suspicion a thing."

Ridey was nodding thoughtfully. "Mebbe. But mebbe not."

"He'll drop his guard. Figuring we're all open and in plain sight."

The old man nodded again. "Except I prefer fightin' my own troubles, mister. So it'll be me takin' a look about."

And before Slocum could say either yes or no, the old man had opened the door and stepped outside. He was empty-handed, save for his holstered six gun.

Standing at the side of the window, Slocum watched Ridey walk slowly toward the barn, then veer off as though he'd thought of something while he headed toward the corral. He stopped for a moment, looking down at the block of salt near the gate, as though still thinking. Then, without looking at the barn, he walked toward it; but when he had almost reached it he stopped, put one hand—his left—in his pocket, looking down at the ground as though again reflecting, and finally he turned and walked back to the house.

He didn't enter right away, but stopped at the woodpile outside and selected an armful of kindling for the cooking stove. Kneeling, he loaded the pieces onto his left arm. Slocum was surprised at the old man's capacity. He was carrying a load that would have been heavy for someone twenty years younger.

Slocum didn't make the mistake of opening the door for him, but instead stood back so that anyone outside would not see him.

"He ain't there," Ridey said as he knelt down and deposited his heavy load. Slocum had noted that he was sweating only a little on his forehead. "There ain't nobody in there."

"Figures," Slocum said.

Ridey Bones was surprised. "How you figger?"

"It's an old hoss apple," Slocum said. "Makin' a play with one hand while you second deal with the other."

"You mean, there really isn't anybody in the barn? Not supposed to be even?"

"Yup."

"But somebody wants us to think there is."

"Yup."

"How so?"

"So we won't wonder where they're really coming from."

"But there is somebody watchin' the outfit."

"There is," Slocum said. "I seen his gun barrel glinting."

"He could pick us off is what you're saying."

"He could but he won't. He's only there to shake us."

"They ain't doin' a very good job," the old man said.

"That's what I think."

The old man threw his head up toward the rimrocks. "Up yonder's where they been wanting to bunch all them beeves."

They seated themselves at the kitchen table after

Ridey Bones brought over the coffee pot and two mugs.

Slocum watched him as they both drank.

"That'll make a man stand up and salute, by God."

"Still got the hair on."

"Well, what we gonna do?" the old man suddenly asked the ceiling.

"Did you check the outhouse when you were out there?"

"I sure did. Far as I can tell there is only that one up there, likely with a Sharps and he's got it sighted to pick us off like how-de-do, for Chrissake." The old man took his hat off roughly and then banged it down on his head again. "I'm for waitin' till it's dark and ridin' up there an' coldcockin' the sonofabitch."

"That's what they want you to do," Slocum said.

Ridey Bones glared at him. "Reckon I am gettin' old," he said, his tone sour. "On the other hand, a man don't ever have to be too old to learn." He sighed then. "Young feller, how long you figger on hanging around this part of the country?"

"Till I git my business done."

The old man lifted his heavy eyebrows at that and stared at Slocum as though asking him what he was doing here.

"When I git done with what I came up here to do in the first place," Slocum repeated. And reaching into his shirt pocket he took out a wooden match and placed the plain end in his mouth, letting it hang from his lip while he contemplated the ceiling of Ridey Bones' log house.

4

John Slocum suddenly realized he had been standing on the wooden boardwalk outside the Generosity Saloon for a good while as all those still very vivid memories went through him. And he knew it was time to move. It was never a good idea to make yourself that easily available to whoever might take a notion to brace you one way or the other. But now quite casually he spotted the young boy who had almost run into him earlier. He was running fast, his yellow hair flying behind him, and Slocum realized he would be coming right by him again. Somehow he knew it was time to move on.

Turning, he made his way down to the Best Food Cafe and picked a stool at the end of the counter.

The geezer in the greasy apron nodded. "What'll it be?"

"Coffee. Then I'll see."

The cafe was almost deserted.

At the counter two men were eating steaks, the usual breakfast at that time of day. And John Slocum saw no reason why he shouldn't do the same. But he picked a table to sit at, wanting to be alone with his thoughts.

It was easy enough to figure out why someone would want Ridey Bones' Double C spread. The graze was prime and the whole layout was high in the mountains. This meant that it carried strong winds, which in the winter would blow the snow so that stock could find their feed. But somehow he felt pretty sure it wasn't for stock raising that the CC range was so aggressively coveted.

Mr. Bones had not been very forthcoming with information, shaking his head in tired exasperation whenever Slocum questioned him. And indeed, as Slocum soon found out, the old boy didn't favor being followed with a mounting succession of questions from the big man with the green eyes. Slocum had come to the conclusion that Ridey was holding something back; and indeed he clearly remembered now that following their confrontation with the gunslingers he had felt the old man somehow closing. Again the vivid memories returned. . . .

Later, following another mug of coffee, and with the women still in the other room, he had brought up again the question of why someone would want the Double C that badly.

And again the old man just wagged his head. "Damned if I know. I got nothing here anybody wants. And like I alre_ady told you, I've allowed them other outfits to come through below Barley Creek when they want to run their stock up on the mountain. Told 'em again and again I got no objection. So, I don't know what in hell them or anybody else would want this outfit for." He spat again and then canted his head toward Slocum. "You got a notion, mister?"

They'd been through it plenty already, and Slocum knew the old boy didn't expect any other answer than he'd already given two, three times. But this time he decided to say something different.

"I am going to ask you something, mister, being as you have felt free and easy 'bout askin' me things, stuff a man might not always cotton to answerin'."

"Like . . . ?" And the old man looked at him, with one eye closed, and with his tongue in his cheek making a ball.

"Like your asking what my personal business might be up in this here country."

Ridey Bones sniffed. "Well, now, like just what is your business up here with all them questions about myself and my neighbors? 'Pears to me a might nosey I must say, Mr. Slocum." And he lowered one eyelid all the way over his red and rheumy eye, while keeping the other wide open.

"I am looking for a man named Otis. I do believe I told you that, mister."

"And I told you I can't help ya."

Slocum got to his feet then. He touched the brim of his Stetson hat with his forefinger. "Then I reckon there ain't much else to put to 'er then." And he started to the door of the cabin.

"Spend the night if you've a mind to, mister," Bones said.

"Should be gettin' to town."

"Sorry I can't help you."

Slocum had his hand on the door latch. "No, you ain't sorry. But I don't take it personal," he said.

At that point a young, female voice suddenly and unexpectedly entered the conversation.

"Mr. Slocum, please be our guest." It was Janey Bones, just entering the room. "Grandma and I couldn't help but hear Grandpa's invitation, and Grandma said please ask you to stay. She also said she's sorry she is under the weather and can't ask you in person. And I am asking too." And she stopped suddenly, as though startled, her face flushing; delightfully Slocum thought.

"I should be riding on, miss, but if it's all right, maybe I could accept your invite." And he hoped the color wasn't rising in his neck, as he felt it might be when she smiled at him.

She was, he told himself, the best looking thing he'd seen in this good long while. And he always remembered the old saying that all work and no play could make John Slocum a dull boy.

He threw his bedroll in the bunkhouse, per his host's offer. And he retired early, right after supper with Ridey and the girl, who had left early to help her grandmother, who was bedridden with some kind of stomach ailment.

It was quiet in the bunkhouse, which was just off the north end of the barn. And he was glad to see that there was no moon, for he wanted to walk about a bit and explore the place. He still had this feeling—indeed he'd had it all along—that Ridey Bones was keeping something from him. Why were the Rhine bunch hassling him? He could see no reason why the Double C itself would be of special value to the bigger outfit, or indeed to anyone else in that section of the country.

He didn't feel like turning in yet, so he took another turn around the periphery of the house and outbuildings. He was just about to enter the bunkhouse again when he heard her. Her voice was soft, and he instantly felt how suitable her tone was to the night that was warm, yet by no means hot; starlit, though holding a man's privacy with all its softness.

"Mr. Slocum? Is that you?" Her voice was just low enough so that he knew it wasn't going to carry any further than the two of them.

"What a surprise," Slocum said. "I was thinking of taking a little walk. Would you join me?"

"I wanted to talk to you."

"We could do both."

"Of course."

They spent a few moments in silence, while he felt her closeness.

"Mr. Slocum, I feel I am trespassing on you, but I simply have to find someone I can talk to. It's about Grandpa."

"You're worried about him."

"I heard those men who rode up and threatened Grandpa."

They crossed the area behind the house now and were out beyond the horse corral.

"If we could talk. Well, I'd like to offer you a cup of coffee only we might wake up . . ." She let it hang. "Everybody's gone to bed."

And the next thing he realized he had his arms around her. Her lips were soft, eager, her breath was warm, and her body clung to every curve of his.

"Oh, my God . . . my God . . ." But he covered her mouth with kisses.

Now the moon was risen and light bathed the clearing where they walked. They were just out of sight of the house and barn but it was totally private as far as he could tell.

He realized instantly that the bond that had brought them so swiftly together was as strong and as certain as a roping horseman and roped calf. The sole difference was that the calf struggled to be free, while in this instance Slocum—to his delight—realized that the girl was struggling only to be next to him and as swiftly as possible.

In moments they were both naked and he laid her on her back on top of their mixed clothing. They were both gasping for breath as the fire surged through them, flaming them as one single, undulating body. She was soaking wet as his stiff erection stroked in and out, up and down, slowly and quickly, riding her high, low, and every possible which way to bring the two of them to the ultimate ecstasy before exploding in great squirts of liquid passion. Slocum thought he would lose his mind. Never—never!—had he experienced such passion, such a peak of unutterably mixed agony and bliss to the excruciating instant when he could hold back no longer and he came in great rushing, stroking, squirming, and twitching shots of come. She cried out, though her cries were muffled in his ear as she writhed on his massive organ, taking it all the way in until it would go no further, and riding it like a great stick—which, of course, it was. As she murmured and whispered and cried out and dug her fingernails into his bare back and buttocks, she reached down and squeezed his balls until every drop had come.

They lay in each other's arms, exhausted, their legs still entwined, his organ totally limp, empty, satiated with the ultimate delight.

"Thank you," he said softly in her ear. "That was great."

"My pleasure," she murmured and bit his earlobe lightly.

He leaned up on his elbow and looked down into her face, the outline of which was not too clear, even with some light coming from the moon. And he realized she was a girl with a sense of humor.

"I'd like to get to know you," he said, with a teasing smile in his voice.

"Well, I believe you've made a start," she said.

"A good one, I trust."

"I'll let you know," she said. "I need to think it over."

"Why don't we try it over," he said, reaching down between her legs to slip his finger into her already eager slit.

She was soaking, and already her buttocks were undulating under his exploring finger.

"Oh, God," she murmured, "oh my God . . ."

This time he turned her over onto her hands and knees, and in a trice had driven his hammering organ right up into the middle of her whole body, to the very root of her sex.

She was whimpering with delight as he worked his great cock round and round, then sliding it almost all the way out, and holding it there until he thought he would come. Still he held it, then slid it slowly in all the way in a slow, carefully measured stroke, then out and in again, each time increasing the exquisite tempo until they were both moving faster and faster. His eager hands reached under her and held her teats, squeezing and stroking as he worked deeper and deeper into her, and then swifter, as they both were soaking with their lovemaking and again they came as she cried out, begging him for the ultimate squeeze and squirt of his passion. Their timing was as one as they reached the ultimate instant of their desire and satiation, then they collapsed, almost sobbing with joy and relief.

She turned back to face him then and they lay wrapped in each other's arms. They slept.

5

He smiled as he remembered that night, slowly bringing himself back to the present. But so far he still had not found any link to Otis. But why had Finnegan pointed him toward Finality Gulch? He had nosed about in more than just the two main saloons, not hearing a word, not picking up on any interest or any kind of look from any of the hangers-on. Otis. He might as well have mentioned George Washington for all the reaction he got.

Yet to be sure it was what he'd expected. He knew very well that nobody was going to come forward and offer information on such a man. He knew he was making himself a target by even mentioning the name. But it was the only way, he knew. He had deliberately made himself a target by asking about the man who was his quarry—and Finnegan's target. Any other way, not knowing the country or its people, would have taken him into too many dead trails—and big trouble, he was sure.

Well, he reasoned as he started down the street, he had done what he had planned to do. There was nothing more he could do. The only thing now was to wait. He knew that he had definitely made himself a target.

But he also had the very strong feeling that there was something else brewing in Finality Gulch. The town had that smell to it. Trouble. And not small. And, for all he knew right now, he could very easily be the trouble. He had the very strong feeling that Finality Gulch had been waiting for him.

On an impulse he suddenly turned off the street and pushed through the swinging doors of the Silver Dollar Saloon. He recognized the beefy man behind the bar, an old-timer who had served drinks at the Pastime down in Douglas. That had been two or three years back. Neither Slocum nor the beefy server of drinks offered recognition to the other. Good enough, Slocum decided. That was the way it should be. But he knew that he had a chance for an opening. The man knew him, knew his reputation, knew that he'd punched cows down at the Double Swat at Douglas and was no owlhooter. So he moved easily to the bar and ordered a whiskey.

The man behind the long bar was almost totally bald. At first a casual observer might decide he was on the fat side, but a closer study would have revealed that this was an illusion. The bartender—whose name had been Tiny Tom Spokane, at least when he'd been at Douglas—was built of whalebone and steel. Indeed, he'd been a bare-knuckle fighter and some said, had even sparred with Yankee Sullivan, the champion. In any event, Slocum knew he was no man to mess with, though he'd never had reason to cross the beetle-browed bruiser. He knew of others who had, and who had lived—more or less—to tell about it.

Just for a split second, as he pushed the thick glass and bottle in front of his latest customer, Tiny Tom's small eyes threw off a glint of recognition. He nodded slightly. John Slocum took it as a good sign. It was as though someone was with him; for two others in the

Generosity had ignored him, though he read the recognition in their lean faces.

Standing at the bar now, he listened to the whir of the wheel of fortune, the clink of poker chips, and the chanting of the faro dealer. He dropped all thoughts of his failure to learn anything from Ridey Bones about Otis, dropped too his thoughts of the girl, and remembering that there was promise of future action—as she had let him know—he concentrated now on his assignment with Heavy Hank Finnegan.

He knew he didn't have much time. Somehow, even though there had been no obvious connection between his search for Otis and his meeting with Ridey Bones he knew that there had to be something that had drawn him toward both situations. He suddenly remembered Standing Horn, the Oglala chief who had told him that everything was connected. Somehow. And Slocum had that feeling now. It was not chance that had brought both Finnegan and Bones into his life, and himself into theirs. And he was fairly sure that more likely than not Otis and Jake Whistler were in the same pot of mulligan.

He had been leaning with his back to the bar, his elbows up on the railing, while he watched the room casually, not at all in any way that would attract notice.

Immediately in front of him a poker game was in progress. Two cowhands and three older men were seated around the battered table, with drinks and smoke clouding smell and visibility in the already noisy, dimly lighted groups. It was a big room, with a big bar, and there were a half dozen games in progress—not only poker, but faro and a lively dice game.

Suddenly, Slocum realized someone—the big bartender—was behind him, and by turning his head slightly, as though looking for someone across the room, he caught a glimpse of that muscular mastodon. He could hear the soft, wet movement of the bar rag on the mahogany as Tiny Tom Spokane worked his hand over the beer and whiskey slops. At one point, the rag touched Slocum's elbow. He half turned, moving his arm out of the way as, at the same time, he smelled the onion on Tiny Tom's heavy breath.

"Watch yerself."

The words were more breathed than spoken. And it was the intensity of the warning that reached Slocum. For a split second it struck him as strange that the huge bartender would warn him; for though they'd shared a few words in the past, in no way would he have considered himself and Tiny Tom friends. Unless . . .

Unless of course, Tiny had it in for someone, or in for himself, John Slocum. Though why would he have it in for himself? Well, he couldn't take the time to worry about that. The warning was useful no matter who it favored. It also told him what he was beginning to suspect; that his presence was known, maybe even well known, and that more than likely he'd even been expected in Finality Gulch.

It made a difference, for sure. No matter why, or by whom, the point was that he'd been targeted; and he suspected it could have happened even before he reached Finality, maybe even back at Ridey's Double C, maybe way back in Ten Town. With a sonofabitch such as Heavy Hank Finnegan, a man could figure on likely anything.

He didn't have long to wait. He had been partly watching the whole room, partly keeping some attention on the game of stud being played out at the table almost directly in front of him. He turned around from time to time to watch the room in the big mirror in back of the bar. But right now he was leaning back on the bar, on his elbows, watching the poker game being played out with two drovers, and three older men, including the dealer who was a house man.

Slocum had noticed that one of the players, a man of maybe forty-some years in a black frock coat, seated to the right of the dealer, had glanced at him twice, though without any sort of recognition. It could have been quite an idle look, seen often enough during any poker game, or even during random conversation as someone just glances around a room, resting from the talk, the cards, or maybe just looking at nothing to rest the eyes and relax from the concentration of the game. Except, Slocum was sure, the look was more than that.

He couldn't figure out why the man was looking at him. He was an older man, and he'd never seen him before. And it seemed sure that he was no threat in any way. He looked like anything but the type who would pull a gun or a knife.

And then the thought came in like a blade; that he was being set up. The man who had glanced at him was setting him up by catching his attention.

Suddenly an argument broke out at the poker table. The man who had looked at him those two times was being accused of harboring extra aces.

"You slipped that ace, God damn you!" the man seated opposite the dealer said. But he wasn't talking to the dealer, rather the man next to him, the man who had looked twice at Slocum.

In a split second the whole room had stopped.

"You're a liar," the accused man said. "It's you who got extra aces. You're a cheating sonofabitch and you always have been, by damn!"

The attention of the entire room was instantly riveted to the five men at the green baize-top table. And for a flashing instant, Slocum too found himself caught. But some extra sense that was now an innate part of him after all those years on the trail saved him.

Quick as a whistle, he dodged the blow of the club that came down behind him and smashed onto the bar, shattering his glass and a couple of bottles, and spilling whiskey all around. Turning, he jumped up onto the bar and kicked Tiny Tom Spokane squarely in the throat.

Instantly he was down on his feet on the floor and had upended the poker table as the man who'd been eyeing him drew a derringer from inside his coat. A bottle missed him as somebody in the back of the room decided to enlarge the fracas. And now the room was in an uproar of flying fists, feet, curses, shouts, screams, flying bottles, and even a chair which came smashing down on top of the bar, having fallen short of the tempting target of the mirror behind it.

And then it was over. For Slocum, at any rate, who had fought his way to the swinging doors, and quickly stepped outside even as a flying bottle smashed into the wall close enough to his head to spray him with broken glass and booze. Stinking of whiskey, he made his way quickly to The Frontier House where he was staying the night.

There was no bath on his floor, so he fetched water in a bucket and washed himself in the basin in his room. Then he rolled himself a cigarette and lay down on his bed for a smoke, fully clothed. He was, in fact, prepared for visitors.

He didn't have long to wait and was not at all surprised when he heard the steps outside in the hall. And the single knock at his door.

In a trice he was up and on his feet with the Colt .44 in his fist.

"Who are you and what do you want," he demanded, keeping to essentials.

"Clay Byles, town marshal." The voice came hard through the door. "I want to talk to you, Slocum."

Slocum weighed it. The voice was not only hard, but also sure of itself, yet not angry, and he could detect no guile in it. It was to be expected, after all.

"Alone," he said.

"I am alone."

Swiftly he checked the window in case of a second caller at his back. It was late afternoon now and the light was starting to leave the sky just above the high peaks of the mountains that were in full view. He stepped silently to the side of the door and removed the chair that he had propped beneath the knob while he'd bathed. Then he stepped back and to the side out of any line of fire; and with his six gun covering the door, his vision including the window. It wouldn't have been easy for someone to come in that way, they'd have had to be lowered by rope from the roof, but it could be done; and it would require the occupant—himself—to be distracted. Like with a knock at the door.

"Come in."

The door opened and Marshal Clay Byles walked in.

"Shut the door," Slocum said, taking in the stocky man with the broken nose and hairy ears. He did not lower his weapon as he added, "And state your business."

With his eyes on his host the marshal reached back with his foot and kicked the door shut. "That how you always talk to the law, Slocum?"

"It's how I'm talking to you," Slocum said, showing no surprise that the lawman knew him. "After all, how do I know you're a lawman? A lot of gunslingers now and again wear tin."

"Want me to reach for my papers?"

"I do."

The marshal did so, handing a certificate of his status to Slocum, who glanced at it and handed it back.

"Sorry about that, Marshal," he said holstering his gun. "But I had to be sure. Some heavies tried to finish me off in the Generosity Saloon."

"That's why I am here," Byles said.

Slocum motioned the marshal to sit on the bed while he took the one chair, turning it to himself with its back facing Byles, thus giving him a firmer purchase from which to rise as well as a useful weapon in his hand should he feel the need.

He could see that the marshal appreciated the way he was outmaneuvered, and his eyes flicked from Slocum's face to his holstered gun.

Marshal Byles was a short bulldog in his fifties, and though he'd been through just about all of it in his time, he was in no mind to cross that impassive man seated there right in front of him. At the same time, the marshal of Finality Gulch was no chicken either.

"Last time I heard of John Slocum was when he was riding some with Nate Champion."

Neither man moved or spoke for a long moment and the sentence stayed there like another person.

"I don't have no flyer on you," Byles finally said.

"That's what I know," Slocum said.

"I'd like to keep it that way."

"You got any reason not to?"

"What are you doing here is what I want to know."

"Minding my own business."

"Good enough then. But if there's trouble I'll be looking for you."

"How come you got a hard-on, Marshal? You don't know me. And I never heard of you."

"The way you busted up that saloon was enough to hear about you, Slocum."

"I didn't start that trouble."

"But you were the cause of it."

"All I was doing was having a drink at the bar."

"Listen—your being there was enough to start a fight that wrecked the place."

"Was that my fault, for Chrissake!" It was clear that the whole situation had been staged. But by whom? Who would give a damn about his being in Finality Gulch? Otis? Did Otis know of him? And if so, how? He hadn't spoken to anyone other than Ridey Bones. So who had steamed up Byles, with his tin star and his ready six gun?

It occurred to him suddenly to ask Byles about Otis, but then he checked himself. A man like Otis could as well as not have a U.S. marshal on his string. Though Byles, he had to admit, didn't look the sort. Byles looked pretty much to be his own man.

"Be careful," Byles said. "I know you're not in Finality to admire the scenery."

"Who told you?"

"Told me what?"

"That I was coming here."

"Nobody. It's my duty to keep aware of anyone special riding through."

"I wouldn't say I was riding through," Slocum said. "I figured I might do a bit of wrangling up around the North Fork; maybe with Ridey Bones's Double C."

He watched it hit the other man. The lawman's lips tightened, and he canted his head, tipping the brim of his Stetson hat back as he looked about for a place to spit.

Finally, he stood up, walked to the window, opened it and let fly. Then he shut the window and returned to the bed.

"Just don't start any trouble, Slocum. I have heard of you. And this town is trouble-free—so far."

Slocum held his eyes right on the other man, letting his anger cool before he spoke. Then he said, "And if someone else starts it?"

"That ain't likely."

"I'll remember you said that, mister." And Slocum stood up. "If you got nothing else to say, I'm busy."

The marshal rose then. "Good enough," he muttered. He took off his hat and resettled it further over his brow and, with a curt nod to his host, opened the door and left the room.

Slocum stripped down and lay on the bed. He lay awake a long time thinking of what he was going to do, and how, and wondering especially who had arranged the donnybrook at the Generosity. And why. . . .

6

He was an older man, and he looked even older than he actually was. Everybody said it. Quietly though, not to anyone who might pass it on; and for sure not to himself. Not even a hint of age or physical inability could enter a conversation with the old buzzard. A man watched himself right close in the presence of such a person.

Thing was, nobody appeared to know anything much about him; where he'd come from, and like that. He could have been sixty or seventy, but being so stove up, it was hard to tell his actual years. Some said he'd been kicked by a bronc, and maybe even stomped on to boot. Others said it had been a gunfight more than likely, or he'd been beaten. Still, the old boy got about. He'd been in the country a fair while, and he ran a big outfit. But he wasn't at all what anyone would call an old-timer.

Rhine. Bark Rhine. Just over five feet, though he must have been taller when he was young. Now he was bent over—it was the rheumatiz, some said, on top of the injuries. No one knew, and for certain no one was about to ask.

He sat now in the deep leather chair at his desk, but he was not looking at the papers that were in front of him. Actually, he wasn't looking at anything in particular.

There came a knock at the door and his head moved slightly.

"Come." The word sounded like a bark.

The door opened then and a man appeared, bareheaded, and holding his Stetson hat awkwardly in his hand, looking unused to the gesture.

The man at the desk didn't move, nor did he speak.

"There's a rider coming," the visitor said after a moment of waiting in the tightening silence.

"I know that. You think I'm deaf or somethin'?" The eyes were now right on the visitor, pecking all over the man's face. "What's he want?"

"Don't know yet, the outriders first spotted him down by the butte."

"You know him?"

The foreman of the Circle BR moved his head. "No, Mr. Rhine. The men never seen him before." He hesitated then, and the eyes at the desk stabbed at him.

"Why didn't you find out? Why didn't you get one of your men to find out? What am I payin' you men for, fer Chrissakes!"

In the next moment of silence, the foreman stood very still before his angry employer. He was used to it, and not put out by these frequent turns of ill will.

"Ten'll get you twenty it's John Slocum," the man at the desk said. "I've been expecting him." And suddenly he leaned back in his chair and a cackle of laughter broke out of the wrinkled face. "Flies to honey, Jasper. Flies to honey or. . . ." And his small eyes opened wide. "To horseshit. Hah! Eh!" He sniffed wetly and, whipping out a big red bandanna, he blew vigorously into it, then folded it carefully and tucked it back into his hip pocket, leaning over onto the desk and disturbing his papers in order to do so.

"Slocum . . . ?"

"The one who tore up the Generosity."

"I know who you mean," Jasper said. "But how . . . ?" He stopped, puzzled, and also unwilling to again play into his employer's hand.

"Where did you say? Down by Shelley Butte? Hah! He's heading for here more than likely, and/or for Whistletown."

Hendry Jasper suddenly noticed the drop that had formed on the end of Bark Rhine's nose. Try as he might he couldn't stop staring at it, wondering just when it would fall.

"Well . . . ?" The word came out of the figure behind the desk like a file on the edge of a piece of tin. "Don't stand there staring the spots off yer cards—play 'em!"

"Just wonderin' if you'd want me to whistle up some of the boys—for this feller Slocum. I heard how he cleaned out the Generosity. Figure we better be ready for him."

The man at the desk had been doodling with his pencil on a piece of paper, now he leaned back dropping the pencil, and sighed. "Mr. Jasper, I do not want any mistakes made with our visitor. And you had better impress that on your men. I'm not talking just about the cowhands that are regulars here, but the men specially hired ten days ago in expectancy of Mr. Slocum's arrival."

"Huh . . ."

"Do you understand?"

"Yup. Yessir . . ."

"Make sure you do. I will be dealing with Mr. Slocum. Of course, if he should get roughed up on his way here . . ." He shrugged and smiled into the middle distance. "You understand me."

"I do."

"You may go." And he dropped his head to the pad of paper in front of him. Only when he heard the door shut behind his departing foreman did he lift his head.

With a sigh he reached over and tapped the round bell that was resting on top of a book. One—two—three taps.

He was delighted that the response was almost immediate, as he heard the tiny tap on the door.

"Come."

The knob had already started to turn, and Rhine began to feel the familiar stirring inside himself.

"Come in, my dear, and do lock the door behind you." He was leaning forward on the big desk, leaning on his forearms which were making an arch in front of him.

"I hope I'm not interrupting you."

She seemed to him to be smiling everywhere—in her face, her eyes, in her voice, in the way she moved. Dark, with large brown eyes, a wide mouth with full lips, and a figure that burst at her riding habit. Indeed, he thought she looked as though she'd been poured into her black britches and green silk shirt. His eager eyes—as always—felt over every inch of her. And he could tell that she was delighted.

"Sit, my dear."

She had walked casually to the horsehair sofa near the stone fireplace, and now with her fingers lightly touching one of the large arms, she faced him. A smile danced in her eyes—and all around her, he thought. And for an instant he had the strongest impulse to reach for his notebook and write the phrase down. A good one, he decided, and he could use it. But he didn't want to interrupt the moment and so decided to trust his memory.

"My dear," he said. "I only have a moment. I'm expecting company."

Her large eyes seemed to become larger. "But—for all night?"

He chuckled at that, and just narrowly escaped a fit of coughing, managing after two gasps to control himself. "No, my dear. It shouldn't take me long to handle the business. And then. . . ."

"And then . . . ?" Her eyes lifted in amusement as they played their game.

"And then we can—uh—play?" His tight forehead seemed suddenly to loosen as though something extraordinary had surprised him, and he started to chuckle.

He pushed back his chair now, controlling his laughter as she walked around the desk and stood in front of him while he turned his chair, so that she could stand between his parted legs.

She was smiling down at him and he reached out and placed his hands on her buttocks, drawing her to him.

"Boo-boo," she said softly. "I didn't lock the door."

"I know." His breath was coming quicker now as he drew her to him, his hands squeezing her buttocks.

"You don't mind if somebody comes in?"

"I can't know whether I will or not until it happens," he said.

And then she was down on her knees. He already had his cock in his hand, offering it. She didn't hesitate, taking it instantly in her mouth with long, tickling strokes as she fluttered her tongue.

Meanwhile, he was squirming with the ecstasy she always brought him, and at last came and came. Together they collapsed in their usual position; satiated and tired, but joyful at the great flooding and the relief that had followed.

"There'll be more where that came from later," he said after a while as she looked up at him.

"I hope we don't have to wait too long."

"We can look forward to it," he said. And then suddenly, "Why are you looking like that?" And he moved in his chair, dropping his hands from her shoulders.

"I don't know how I was looking at you," she said, and he heard the alarm in her voice.

"You think I'm too old for you . . . that it?"

She shook her head, surprised at him. "Boo-boo, what's the matter? Didn't you like it?"

"Or maybe I'm too . . . well . . . not so handsome as I used to be."

"I don't know how you used to look," she said, and there was worry in her voice. She hated it when he played with her like this.

"I was a real handsome feller in my day," he said, and she caught the sneer in his voice.

"You're real handsome now," she said.

"Only in the dark, my dear," he said and his voice was harsh. Reaching down he buttoned his pants, saying, "Excuse my disgusting self-pity. I guess I just haven't yet gotten used to what happened to me."

"I'd like you to tell me about it some time," she said, still on her knees, looking up at him.

"No you wouldn't. That's something I'll never tell anybody." And then he added, "Not even you."

Rhine! The name was waiting for him as he awakened early. That morning in the big double bed. It was as though the name itself had called him from sleep.

John Slocum had lain there in the pre-dawn wondering why it had suddenly come to him like that. He knew that thoughts and feelings often got connected in that twilight of evening or, even more so, in early morning slumber. You were asleep but at the same time something was awake. It seemed as though the hard core of thought and physical action—even feelings of anger and desire—was at bay. The body was relaxed and open, not taking over to dictate the mind through appetite, fatigue, desire, happiness, or sorrow. There was a place where the guards were not standing sentinel to one's deeper feeling . . . one's deeper knowing.

For he had experienced it on the trail, and now here in the dingy hotel room at the Frontier House in Finality Gulch he felt it again—that opening to something other; that place where feelings run deeper than thought and the mind knows and is in the act of living what it knows.

The bed springs twanged loudly as he shifted his weight. He lay still, listening to the early morning sounds in the street below. It was still dark now, though a pale glimmer of light was on the windowsill. A dog barked. He found his thoughts again on Janey Bones. Funny, how even during a tough time like this you could meet someone quite unique.

He had just started to doze off when a step in the hall outside his room brought him wide awake. At once he was on his feet, just as the knock came at the door.

He stood absolutely still, fully aware of every sound and movement.

"Slocum!" The voice was hard, insistent, but low.

In the weak light coming through the window behind him, he watched the doorknob turn, but luckily he had locked the door when he had come in.

He was just on the point of challenging whoever was there when he heard a sound at his back. Spinning he saw the legs coming down from the window of the room above him. He was across the room and had slammed the barrel of his .44 against the intruder's shin followed by a second smash in the groin. The man let out a scream of pain and, losing his grip, fell like a sack to the street below. Behind Slocum there was a crash as the door burst open.

Three men carried him to the floor, but not before he had delivered some damage with the gun barrel. A tremendous blow in the pit of his stomach knocked out his breath; and suddenly he was on his back on the floor, with somebody's knee against his throat and the point of a knife at his temple.

"Now you get this, Slocum, and you get it good! You ain't wanted in Finality Gulch. You get yer ass outta this town and that means right now! If you know what's good for you, you sonofabitch!"

Although he could barely see the shape of his attackers he could smell them all right. They were well liquored. The speaker leaned real close; Slocum could feel his breath on his ear. "You got that, you sonofabitch?"

Slocum could say nothing; there seemed to be no breath in him at all.

"You got that?" And the knife point pushed hard against the cord in his neck.

He grunted.

"You and your ass get shut of this town come sunup. That's about right now!"

All at once a light went on in a building across the street and he glimpsed the man who had spoken—thick mustache, scar on his left cheek, the reek of forty-rod whiskey whistling through scattered teeth.

"You got it! And remember—Mr. Rhine sends his compliments."

And they were gone.

"I gotcha," he said softly and he continued to lie in a heap on the floor. "And I will not forget you."

After a while—he'd no notion how long it was—he knew his ribs weren't broken, although it felt like it.

Save for some cuts and bruises, he was more or less in one piece. Only thing was he felt as though he'd been tromped by a couple of feisty broncs.

At last he pulled himself up onto the bed and lay there a long time. Suddenly a thought came to him and he began looking for his .44. It was nowhere to be found. Checking further he discovered the Winchester was also missing, leaving him without any weapon at all. As some good while later the sky began to lighten, he felt himself filling with a cold, burning anger.

The first rays of the morning sun were just touching the town as he stepped out onto the street. Actually, he felt better than he thought he should, and this gave him a good feeling all round. He was whistling softly between his teeth as he started down the street.

Right then he spotted the two loungers squatting in the doorway of the Generosity directly across from his hotel.

"Well, I will for sure be gone by sunup," he said to himself as he walked down to the livery barn.

The hostler was up and about, and he discovered to his relief that no one had been near the Appaloosa. It was good seeing the pony wide awake and feisty to get going. John Slocum began to feel better. His anger had cooled, but it hadn't lessened. It was, in fact, exactly how he wanted it. Being too angry would hurt him; he had it now in a place where it would give him the most help.

The hostler assured him that no one had been at the livery to check his horse or duffle that he had left there. He had another .44 in his gear in the duffel behind the cantle on his saddle skirt. But they had taken his Winchester from the hotel room, along with his holstered .44.

It didn't matter. He was going to ride out there anyway. He was that mad.

7

First there had been the trappers and the mountain men, then the gold seekers and buffalo killers. Finally, the cattlemen. To the stockman the cow was the way of life, as the buffalo was for the Indian. From the cow came meat, fat, soap, and candlelight; its skin became clothing, even shelter, the cover for his wagon bows, the rugs in his cabins. And too it provided rawhide for baskets, dough pans, bedsprings, and chairs seats. Rawhide was made into hobbles for horses, and for ropes and lariats. Sometimes it was even used to make nails, for in earlier times it served in place of iron and wood.

The cow, albeit not actually sacred to the white man as the buffalo was to the traditional Indian, was assuredly the westerner's staff of life, especially so for the early Texan; or as the citizens of the new Republic of Texas liked to be called—the Texian.

One of these—though no longer living in Texas—was Ridey Bones. Forty or fifty years back he'd come into his manhood and had done everything with the beeves down on the Panhandle except marry one, as the saying went. Yet he had settled up north in Wyoming.

Ridey Bones had remained "a Texan", even though transplanted to the Powder River country. He had first trailed cattle north with his father, who was now part of the folklore, and had fought the Kiowa, Comanche, and the Sioux. There wasn't much Ridey Bones hadn't been a part of. And from the moment he had ridden into the Powder River country all those years ago he had known this was the place for him to build his brand.

A number of people had not agreed with him. First it was the Indians, then the outlaws, and various cattlemen, and finally the law. When the boot began to pinch, Ridey found he had to make a choice. For then came the damn farmers and homesteaders, the sodbusters. A stupid law it was, the Homestead Act. The damn government giving away free land like that. For a time he'd found a way around it. Stake a fiddle-footed cowpoke and he'd prove up on a 640-acre section of land and sell it back to you. Well, he'd done that not just once but a couple of times.

But then he'd found somebody else was doing the same thing, someone with more money, maybe with the Association behind him. Rhine. Rhine had money in depth, and when the big Die-Up hit all over the West, everybody sold out—if they could. Except Ridey Bones had managed to stick it out; though having to sell off two big sections of good graze; two sections that eventually ended up with Rhine's BR brand. It didn't take much in the way of arithmetic to figure he was surrounded.

Except it was the Double C that kept him in business. It was his old pal Jake Whistler, who he'd ridden with during the war, going up against the likes of Quantrill, by God. And living to tell about it. Then after the war, Jake had built the Whistler gang. Now and again Ridey had looked the other way when Whistler's boys had wintered in the mountains above the Double C. He'd even kept silent when they ran beef into one of the many draws and swiftly—and expertly—changed brands with that handy running iron. Jake had saved Ridey's bacon during the war at one time, and Ridey Bones wasn't a man to forget such a thing. Plus, he was feeling the squeeze from Rhine gobbling up all the Greybull grass he could get his goddamn greedy paws on.

One way or another, with help here and there from Jake in the form of payment for hiding out in the rimrocks and box canyons above the Double C, Ridey had kept his outfit together. And he'd been able to take care of Millie who'd been taken sick this good while, and wasn't much at getting about. Ridey Bones had managed.

But then suddenly—like one of those summer thunderstorms that come up from nowhere and hit, then take off—Jake Whistler was shot and killed. Dry-gulched. Backshot. Murdered with a .30 bullet between his shoulder blades.

There'd been no legal proof on it, but everyone knew it had been Otis, one of Rhine's tough boys. And that more than likely Rhine had ordered it. The wonder was—Ridey would now and again think—that he himself hadn't also been killed. Though, with it all pointing to Rhine, Ridey figured that sonofabitch was likely thinking about some kind of good relations with the local people. Even Rhine couldn't push too far. Best thing, Ridey figured, was for himself and Millie to pull up stakes and get out of the country. But where? There was no place to go and he was flat busted broke. So he did what he saw was the only thing he could do. He stayed. It was, by God, his country anyway; and so he stayed.

Then Otis got taken by the law on another shooting and was doing time in Laramie.

Then one day the girl had shown up.

It had been simple enough to ride out of town as though he were heading east, and then make a wide circle back, pointing finally in the opposite direction. Slocum knew they were watching, and he pretended to be indecisive, as well as in poorer physical shape than he actually was. He told himself he was lucky to feel as strong as he did after that get-together in his hotel room. And he was careful not to bring his handgun out of the bedroll tied onto his saddle skirt. He wanted those hard outriders to think that he was unarmed, and even hurting from the fight. He did have his buffalo-skinning knife close at hand but that was no use except at close range. Still, it was the way the cards lay. And he had learned the hard way early in life that you played them as they lay.

Riding up from Goose Creek now, past the big butte and out in full view of the BR, he knew he could be picked off as easy as swatting a deer fly. But it was the time for boldness, and Rhine had taken the trouble to order him out of the country. So he was counting on the man's curiosity to keep him alive.

Now the sun was up and he could feel it on his back and, when he leaned forward, on the back of his neck. He was chewing a generous plug of tobacco and this caused him to spit a goodly bit. He wasn't a regular tobacco chewer. It was just now and again when he wanted to turn things over in his mind he found the chewing helped.

Just now his eye caught a rider off to the left slipping out of view down a draw. To his right another was briefly outlined. When he reached the stand of box elders and dropped from sight of the ranch houses he felt more at ease, although he knew he was still being watched. It was a strange moment to lose his tension like that, but he had no time to concern himself. Now he quickened the gait of the Appaloosa, rode up a shallow draw, and came suddenly right onto the BR's bunkhouse.

Slocum cussed that swiftness, but only lightly. It was unexpected, and he knew that of course that was why the cabin had been built in that place. But he also knew that it was just the unexpected that a man had to expect.

He began whistling a ditty to himself as a half dozen men came out of the bunkhouse and stood facing him with their hands close to their weaponed hips.

Slocum felt the grin coming into his face. He was in a tight spot for sure, and it was just the way he liked it. He was still whistling softly to himself, just on his breath, whistling between his teeth as he looked down at those six stony faces.

"What you want, mister?" A tall, wide-shouldered man with hair almost down to his shoulders, asked through tightened lips.

"I've come to call on Mr. Rhine," Slocum said, and leaning forward he spat a streak of tobacco juice over the Appaloosa's withers, right into a clump of fresh horse manure. "But first I am looking for a sonofabitch with a scar on the left side of his face who told me Mister Rhine was inviting me to leave the country. I do believe he was wearing some crotch hair on his upper lip." And he turned an icy smile on the hard cowhands.

"I'd be careful of that kind of talk around here, mister," the long-haired cowboy said. "We don't cotton to such, do we, boys?"

A ripple of coarse laughter ran through the group at those words.

Slocum eased himself in his stock saddle. "Sorry, mister. I should've said goddamn sonofabitch." And his eyes were like green stones as he looked right at the long-haired man. "Where is he?"

"Right here," a voice said.

The man had just stepped through the open door of the bunkhouse. He was short, dark, hard-looking, wearing a very tight shirt, and had his right hand very close to the six gun at his hip. He wore a trimmed mustache and a cold smile, and there was a scar running down his right cheek. He also wore a cold smile and the six gun at his right hip was tied-down and low.

Slocum leaned forward, with his forearm on the pommel of his saddle, still whistling softly to himself, but loud enough so the men nearest him could hear. "I reckon you are," he said.

The man in the doorway suddenly laughed. "I hope you got some backup for your fancy talk, mister." He took a step forward and stood facing Slocum and the Appaloosa squarely.

Slocum spat in the direction of the other man's feet almost hitting him. He watched the color fill the other's face and caught the glitter in the man's eyes.

"Maybe you should get down off that hoss, mister."

Slocum grinned at him as he moved back in his saddle, lifting his forearms from his saddle pommel. He reached up and lifted his Stetson hat and resettled it on his head. Whistling almost without any sound at all, he swung down from his saddle. He spat again, not in any particular direction this time.

The man standing in front of him moved into a stance from which he would have his best draw; his right hand and arm out, his legs distanced for quick movement. "Shit, you got no gun," he snapped. "What the hell you doin' among the men, sonny!"

The whole group snickered and one or two guffawed at that.

"I don't have no gun, sir," Slocum said, his eyes big and round with innocence, his voice soft and friendly as he started to walk toward the other.

"A gunhawk without a gun. The famous Slocum not packin' a gun for his backshootin'! How about that, boys!"

Slocum was still moving forward. "Some pigs swiped my gun, and the stores ain't open in town this time of day, so I figured I'd ride out to this here friendly place and see if there might be an extra." He kept right on walking toward the man with the scar as he spoke. "Maybe you could let me have yours."

It was the sheer impertinence that did it. For an instant—less than a breath—the man standing in front of the open door of the bunkhouse was caught in astonishment; Slocum hadn't stopped talking all the time he was walking toward him. And now he was right there, right on top of him. Without breaking his stride, Slocum kicked him just on his kneecap. The man with the scar and mustache let out a scream of pain and almost fell, doubling forward. Slocum simply followed up with his fist chopping like an axe just behind the other man's ear. Even before the man hit the ground, Slocum had reached over and yanked that six gun out of its holster and was covering the astonished group.

"I will talk to Mr. Rhine right now," he said, and kneeling with the gun still covering the group, he removed the former gun owner's gun belt and holster.

He straightened up, a hard smile in his face, his eyes carefully watching the group's breathing. Nobody said a word; they were all caught up in their vast astonishment.

"You on the end." Slocum moved the gun. "Take me to Rhine. And you others, don't forget I got him."

Bark Rhine was standing at the window as Slocum entered his office. He had seen the action outside the bunkhouse. Now the two men faced each other, neither speaking a word. Slocum stood easy halfway into the large room, and Rhine stood with his fingertips pressed hard on the back of his arm chair.

At length Rhine said, "I could have had you killed a dozen times."

"Excepting you didn't."

"I can't promise to control that crew, Slocum, not after the way you mauled them."

"I was easy on them."

Rhine's eyes narrowed, as though he was finding difficulty in explaining something. "Mister, those boys out there do not like you."

Slocum stared at him. He pursed his lips with a frown, reached up and rubbed the back of his neck, and shifted his stance. Then he stood there swing-hipped with his thumbs hooked into his belt and looked at his host with an expression on his face that could only be described as sheepish.

"Gee whiz, Mr. Rhine. I mean . . . like, shucks. I never gave that a thought. Never could have figured how come those real sweet fellers didn't like me. I mean . . . well, all I can say is . . . Shucks . . ." And his eyes widened as he looked at the other man with the hurt innocence of a wrongly accused angel.

The tableau was held by the pair of them for just about thirty seconds and then Rhine broke the silence. A cackle, which Slocum took to be at any rate, a sign of amusement—burst out of him. It popped right out of his mouth like a little ball.

And then all at once he coughed. He seemed to be losing breath as his face reddened. He started to move his arm, as though searching for air. At length he spun his chair around and sat in it, shaking and sucking air as though it was his last chance. Finally, he regained his breath and became still, looking across the wide desk at Slocum, who had helped himself to a seat, pulling it around to the side of the desk.

"I do believe," Slocum said quietly, "that I must've said something funny. Anyways, I have caught your drift. Now what I want to know is where I can find a feller named Otis."

8

He remembered the day like it had been yesterday. Even right now. Standing in the corral outside the barn Ridey Bones again relived that moment he knew he would never forget. Not as long as he lived, which for that matter, he didn't reckon would be all that much longer.

It had been a half year ago. Sometimes it seemed a shorter time, sometimes a whole helluva lot longer. And he spat at a pile of fresh horse manure hitting it plumb center, but not really noticing too much on account of his thoughts being on the girl. That morning she'd come riding up from the river, setting pretty stiff on the little blue roan which he found out later she'd rented from Bill Overs, the hostler down in Finality Gulch.

She was no hand with a horse and he remembered now how he'd somehow been relieved when he'd gotten over his surprise—relieved that old Bill had rented her the roan, who was getting close to making it for crow bait, and not some feisty animal she couldn't have handled, being a greener for sure.

He could tell how sore she was when she drew rein

and winced, trying to cover it as she looked down at him. He'd just gotten back from checking fence and resetting a couple of posts and was leaning a bit on his long-handled shovel, with his other hand holding his fencing tool. And he remembered too—as he had more than once or twice since—how she'd reminded him of something or maybe someone. But he'd not been able to carry that further, not then.

She'd ridden right into the corral where he was standing, and without her drawing rein the pony stopped and swung his head down, like he was relieved that the ride was over. It was a long way up to the outfit from down by the wooden bridge and the river.

Ridey sniffed, relieved that it wasn't one of the riders he had sort of been expecting.

He nodded at the girl, who must have been in her twenties. She still appeared to be having a tough time with the roan. He knew that it wasn't the roan's fault that the girl did not know how to handle a horse.

"What can I do for you, young lady?" Ridey asked. And as he studied the girl he felt something again stirring in him. His alertness instantly returned, spurred by a sense of uneasiness, even danger. There was something strange about her, and at the same time something almost familiar. Especially when she had climbed down from the stock saddle and stood there looking at him with her hands at her waist, almost touching each other. She stood easy, but solid too, her brown eyes steady and clear and giving full attention to the man she was looking at.

"I am looking for a man named Bones," she said then. "They told me in town to come here, above the bridge on the other side of the river. Mr. Ridey Bones."

Ridey remembered how his thoughts had touched the uneasiness in him and he'd tried to find words for it. For sure the girl wasn't looking for a haying job, or chore-boying, or working cattle. His eyes moved past his visitor to the far white peaks of the Absarokas, and the uneasiness swept him again.

"You see anyone on your way up here, miss? Any riders?"

"No. Why no." She shook her head and the sun seemed to flash on her brown hair, visible under the brim of her big hat.

And again something swept through him, a kind of— fear was it? He didn't try to answer, or even to question it. And he realized how reluctant he was to reply to her opening question.

"Where you from?" Ridey asked then.

"Back east. I came out here looking for this man Bones, like I said." And then she added, "From Springfield. From Illinois."

The uneasiness in Ridey began to have a voice. He looked toward the log house, suddenly remembering the spring he and Jake Whistler had dug.

"That's a long piece of travelin'," Ridey said then. "To see somebody." And he hadn't been able to resist asking, "What you want with him?"

Her cheeks had colored then. And she said, "When I see him I'll tell him." She was respectful and she had dignity, which made his uneasiness mount.

Ridey's eyes went to the cabin again. With his game left hand he scratched the stubble on his big, square jaw. He saw the girl's eyes go to his hand; the fingers were bent permanently to the palm. The hand was a claw. And he was thinking of Jake Whistler lying in the mud of Finality Gulch with a bullet in his back, and himself with a bullet through his gun hand, his left. They hunted the killer for more than a week with the biggest posse ever formed in that part of the country. Long ago, it was. Long time. And the whole of the territory had been up in arms over the murder of one of the West's most famous gunmen.

And he could still hear how Otis had promised to come back from prison and finish him off—Jake Whistler's right-hand man.

And he could hear Whistler saying it just like it was right here and right now: "Man with a gun never retires, no matter what side of the law. He dies like he lived, by God."

With his hand shot up Ridey had retired. But now all these years later with Otis just escaped from Laramie, well—he'd likely see if Jake Whistler's statement would hold true. And somehow something in him knew there was more than half a chance it would.

"I am Ridey Bones," he said at last, and he watched it hit the girl. "What's your name, miss?"

"Jane Sturgis. Folks call me Janey."

"What can I do for you?"

What the girl said then was no simpler or direct than he had expected.

"Did you know my father?"

Ridey had looked quietly at the girl then, studying the answer he would give. Then he said, "Can't say as how I ever knowed a man name of Sturgis."

"Maybe fifteen or twenty years ago. A long time. I'm not sure just when."

Ridey spat gently onto the hard-packed ground of the corral. "Nope." His eyes held the girl's.

They looked at each other for a long moment. Ridey saw that the girl was weighing him, not sure his answer was the truth.

"I have come a long way looking for you," she said then. "I wanted to talk to somebody who knew my father. I was told he used to live out here. But I never saw him, not that I can remember,"

Ridey had been looking down to where the bridge

was crossing the river, though hidden from view. His eyes swung back to the girl.

"How come you figured I knowed your pa?"

"I was told somewhere that he knew a man named Bones."

"There are others with that name."

"Not around this part of the country; at least so I have been told."

"I don't recollect that name—Sturgis."

The girl shoved her hands into the pockets or her denim trousers. "Maybe his name wasn't Sturgis then. I've been thinking about that. They told me in town—in Finality Gulch—you used to be a marshal a long time ago. I figured you'd know a lot of names. Maybe you'd remember him."

Ridey shook his head slowly from side to side. "No. I don't recollect anybody name of Sturgis." Then he cocked his head, studying the girl a minute. "What about your ma? She still about? Or some relative?"

The girl shoved her hands deeper into her pockets. "My ma died a year ago. I worked a year saving money to come out here." And she added, "I don't know about any relatives. I just remember the name Bones and this place, Finality Gulch. Funny name, I always thought."

"Yeah," Ridey said thoughtfully. "It's a funny name."

"I was wondering. Maybe . . . maybe he had a different name then. My dad. I've been thinking about that. I have heard of people—men—going out West and changing their names; starting life over, sort of like. Maybe he did that. Maybe his name wasn't Sturgis when he was out here. Maybe you knew him by another name. You see what I mean."

Ridey felt the desperation in her voice and saw it in her eyes as they searched him.

"Did you check with the marshal in town?" he asked.

She nodded. And he looked at her bowed head, knowing that she was choking back tears.

"He was no help. Except telling me where to find you. I just remember that name. Your name. Bones."

"Ridey Bones, was it?"

"I don't remember any other name. Only Bones, and I'm not even sure when or how I heard it." She stopped suddenly, frowning. "Yes . . . yes, when Mom was so sick, before she died. I heard her saying the name. Ridey. Ridey Bones . . . And then she mentioned my dad's name. Jake. Jake Sturgis would be his name. Though . . . although maybe it was different then. It must have been a good long while ago. And she mentioned Finality Gulch. A couple of times."

Then Ridey asked her if her mother hadn't told her something more about her father.

The girl looked down at the ground, then at Ridey; and then she looked away again. He saw the tears sparkling in her eyes.

"She never talked about my dad. Never. And she seemed never to want me to either. It was just that time I heard her talking to Uncle Jack. They didn't know I was in the next room with the door open and I couldn't help hearing. They were saying something about the time Mom and Dad were living out West, out here, and I heard the name Ridey Bones and Finality Gulch."

"Could be your pa wanted it that way too," he said. "I mean, your not knowing about him."

"I don't even know for sure whether he's alive or dead. Maybe he's still alive."

Ridey remembered how they fell silent then, the girl's question and his own refusal lying stiff between them.

He was about to speak again, not knowing at all what to say, but feeling a strong need to comfort the girl. He was just turning in his mind toward Millie, wondering if she could maybe help, when the kitchen door opened and there she was; calling that there was coffee and baking powder biscuits and why didn't they come inside and talk instead of standing there like the two of them didn't know whether to go east or west.

It was enough to relax the moment and both Ridey and the girl laughed. But when they went into the house he quickly took Millie aside and explained to her what had happened. And he swore her to silence at least until the two of them had time to think it out.

"Jake made me promise," he said again and again as he told her who the girl was and what had happened.

"But Jake's dead, and that's his daughter. You can't . . ."

But he cut her off hard. "Not with Otis about." And immediately he could have bitten off his own tongue.

"Otis? you mean that . . ."

"I do. He's busted out, and I know he'll be heading here." Millie looked down at her hands then. "Ride, we've got to keep the girl here, as long as Otis is about. If you send her off, she'll ask around town and you know what will happen. That man Otis I've heard is a madman. He'll find her."

They stood there silently then, looking at each other. They could hear the girl out in the kitchen.

"How?" Ridey asked.

"I'll tell her I need her and she can stay here while we look into the whole thing. See if we can get a line on her dad. You sure she's . . ."

Ridey nodded. "Good enough," he said, and he felt a load leaving him. Although not completely. For he knew—and he knew Millie knew just as well as he did—that more sooner than later they were going to have to tell their visitor the truth.

And he remembered now as he relived those tense

hours that it somehow had worked. She had taken an instant liking to them, and when they said they would help her find out what they could about her father, that they thought they might think of somebody who might be able to help in the search, then she agreed to stay.

Then, later that night Ridey and Millie both spoke to her about the cattle wars, the bandits, the highwaymen, and the generally hard life in the West, especially now around Finality Gulch, adding to the story for emphasis on caution and even secretiveness that there was the likelihood of a gold strike and that everyone had to be careful because of the excitement such an event always whipped up: the excitement of gold which brought the gold seekers and the highwaymen.

Millie didn't like the lie, but Ridey insisted. He explained to her that something strong like that would be the only way to cover the fact—at least for the present—that her father had been just that . . . a highwayman, a train robber, a bank and stagecoach robber, and a cattle and horse rustler. In fact, a notorious gunman.

Sunlight was dancing on the empty glass that stood almost at the edge of the big desk. Slocum watched it, but more of his attention was on the man seated in the big chair, with his back to the window, and the sun that was lighting up the big room.

"I don't happen to know anybody by the name Otis," Bark Rhine was saying.

"Could be you know the gent by another name," Slocum pointed out.

"Can't help you there, mister. I get all kinds of help coming through here, and it's my foreman who could perhaps help you find your man. What was his name? Ovis? Oscis?" He shook his head slowly, and released a long, slow breath.

He leaned forward. "The point is, Slocum, that I am prepared to put you on my payroll, at a pretty good amount. I have heard of you from time to time, but now actually seeing you in action ... like last night, though somebody made a stupid mistake and he will pay for it, I assure you. Last night was, well, you might see it as a test. I wanted to be sure you were all I had heard you to be."

"So ... ?" Slocum cocked his head to one side, his face hard and cold, with his eyes boring into the man at the desk.

"So what else, you're thinking," Rhine said with swift ease.

"I am not interested. And the reason I came out here is to tell you to keep your men off me."

"Or what?" And Bark Rhine was grinning from ear to ear.

At which point Slocum picked up the glass of whiskey and threw its contents in his face.

For an instant Slocum thought the man was going to get up, call out, maybe even reach for a stashed weapon around his desk, but Rhine did none of these things. He sat back in his chair, wiping the whiskey from his red face with a large white handkerchief.

"What a waste of good whiskey. You are indeed a brute, Slocum. That was not trail whiskey, not the rotgut you drink in the western saloons; that was the best scotch whiskey that money can buy. I have it sent from Glasgow by the case." He regarded Slocum with disgust. "You savage!" And then suddenly a grin swept across his face, and his eyes sparkled as though he'd made some sudden magnificent discovery.

"By George, you are indeed the man I want!" He held up his hand swiftly in anticipation of Slocum's objection. "Wait! Hear me out! I need you, Slocum. I seem to be getting nowhere with the brute idiots I have here at the ranch. I need someone with some sense and, let me add, integrity. Honesty," he added.

"Jesus H. Christ . . ." John Slocum breathed the words. He lifted his eyes toward the ceiling in mock piety. "You are breaking my heart, mister. I dunno if I can stand it."

His host's rather large eyeteeth suddenly appeared as he grinned at those words. To Slocum he looked funny and mad at the same time. But he neither grinned nor in fact reacted in any way. For a moment both remained silent.

At length it was Rhine who spoke. "The deity will be of small help with the enterprise I am in the process of getting together, Slocum, and in which I see you as a not small contributor. And it will be—uh—to your advantage. I am happy to say that my source, my informant on your character and your abilities in handling tough situations, did not exaggerate. Indeed, he failed rather to do you justice. In point of fact I am more than thrilled at meeting you and seeing you in action." He leaned back in his chair, which gave a loud crack under the sudden shift in weight.

Now, with his elbows on the arms of the chair, his long fingers formed an arch in front of his chubby body as he regarded John Slocum.

There was evidence of not the slightest reaction from his visitor at this point. Slocum simply looked at him, as he might at something strange he'd only rarely come across, or maybe never at all. Yet, Slocum could well feel the danger of the man. He had met a number of tough operators in his life; men who did their business from a saddle or behind a six gun, or even, as his host of the moment, from a desk. But he had never met anyone quite like Bark Rhine. The man seemed to be none of the sort he'd met and yet at the same time he appeared a combination of all types. Slocum could see him behind a gun, behind a deck of cards, behind a gang of gunslingers, behind a desk, as right now, dealing his deals with only one aim: to win. What was it, though? More exactly? Slocum thought of a snake, a rat, an army of gunslingers, a man with no blood, no feeling even for the power he seemed wholly concerned with. And he remembered now—all at once as he sat in the big leather armchair—he remembered that he *had* heard of Bark Rhine. A man who dealt only stacked decks, who ordered killings, who had ruined ranchers, bankers, land operators and government officials throughout the West. A man who was no more to be trusted than a wounded rattler.

Mr. Rhine meanwhile was leaning an elbow on the arm of his chair and turning the big cigar in his mouth with his forefinger and thumb, as he sucked it and smoked it apparently at the same time. His eyes, Slocum realized, were as cold, hard, and deadly as a pair of bullets precisely on target.

"And I have heard of you," Slocum said now, easing to his feet. He took his time and spoke with his eyes directly on Rhine, driving his attention, his words, his whole self right into the man on the other side of the big desk.

"Good things I'm sure." The smile was careful.

"I trust you as far as I can throw that nice stud horse you got in your round corral just down a piece."

"How did you guess he was mine?" And suddenly he was smiling all over himself, all over the room, and all over Slocum. Slocum had hit his weak spot, just as he'd been trying to do. He grinned himself, letting his host have the moment.

"That's Fire! The best damn pony I ever rode!" He stood up then, and leaning forward a little, placed his fingertips on the edge of the desk. "You might not think I look like a horseman—I've had a couple of accidents in my life—but I would surprise you." He stepped back, lifting his fingers from the desk, but keeping them spread apart, then he leaned down again, harder this time. "I'd like to make you a gift of Fire, Mr. Slocum. I can see you're a lover of fine horseflesh."

Slocum said nothing.

And then Rhine picked up on the silence. "I see you haven't yet made up your mind to accept my offer. You need time. I can give you a little time. Remember, I have an unfortunate habit, Slocum. A habit that sometimes irritates some of the people I work with. Shall I tell you what it is?" He regarded Slocum archly, but didn't wait for an answer, realizing very likely that he wasn't going to get one.

"I always get my way. I am a patient man, to be sure. But only up to a point. Beyond that, I am not patient especially when I realize that my suggestion is not even being considered. Now I am going to run the risk of irritating you, I'm afraid. But . . ." He opened his hands in an offering gesture. "There appears to be no other avenue for getting across my point. I expect to have my way; that is, I shall expect you to take at the most a day, and then you will let me know that you agree to join my—er—my enterprise." He had a huge grin all over his face, and even though Slocum was in no way going to interrupt him, he held up his hand, to stay any remark at all.

His tone was soft, even a little on the jolly side as he said casually, "I'm so happy that you met my—shall I call them neighbors? The—er—Bones family. I am very fond of the Boneses. And I just want to say that out here, out here at Finality Gulch and the surrounding country, we all stand by one another. We help our neighbors. And I especially feel neighborly toward Mr. and Mrs. Bones—Ridey and Millie, whom you've met.

And not to forget their—uh—visitor from back east, Miss Jane Sturgis."

Slocum did not miss the ice in those last words. And as he left the big house and walked toward the Appaloosa who stood patiently at the hitchrail, kicking at an occasional deerfly or biting at tick now and then, he wondered about Bones and the girl. He had felt something more than his own great sexual urge when he was with Janey. There was something more than he could put into words. A sweetness, a softness, an honesty, and a certain innocence. Suddenly he knew what he had only vaguely suspected when he was at the Double C with the Bones and the girl: there was a mystery about her. And he would have bet more than plenty that the girl was in trouble and much more than likely didn't know it.

9

Riding away from the Circle BR, as the ranch houses receded into his backtrail, Slocum found himself with a feeling of unease. Sure, the meeting had gone as he'd expected. Rhine had made his offer—his demand—and he, Slocum, had firmly rejected it. There had to be no question in Rhine's mind that Slocum was not going to be any part of whatever he was up to. Rhine was nobody's fool, and surely he'd gotten the point.

So what was it? Slocum tried to figure out what was bothering him. Yes, nagging at him.

Nothing actually in the conversation itself had troubled him; he had no doubts or questions. But something in Rhine's manner disturbed him, was it his overconfidence? He'd shown a certain sureness in the face of Slocum's hard refusal to have any part of the man's plan, as Rhine himself had put it. His "Big Plan."

Except that he had given up so easily. Rhine had offered no pressure, no threat. He had listened to Slocum say he wouldn't work with him and had not even raised an eyebrow. It was as though he knew something more that Slocum didn't know. He was a man of supreme arrogance, no question about that. For he hadn't argued it. He had simply swept on with his conversation as though Slocum had made not the slightest objection. It was . . . well, it was like he had another plan already in mind, even perhaps already in motion, and there was therefore no question but that Slocum would be a part of it. And for a moment John Slocum felt a sweep of anger going through him. But he let it go. This was no time to allow himself the luxury of losing his temper. He had to keep cool and collected, so he could see just what it was that he was looking at and not seeing.

He pointed the Appaloosa north and west, but did not head for Finality Gulch as he had planned earlier. Instead—he was not sure just why—he found himself riding toward Ridey Bones' Double C. Catching himself up as he rounded a big butte and came in sight of the Greybull rushing south he realized again the strategy so inherent in Bark Rhine. He was definitely a man of roles. And the final one, as he had started to leave, had been that of the hospitable host. He had stretched himself to get Slocum to stay, to linger, turning on his most engaging manner. It had been a great performance. Slocum gave him credit for that. But the question had been why? And because of the circumstances, because it had been Slocum who had initiated the confrontation with Rhine, it was not so clear. Until he realized that while he had taken the initial action to confront the man, it was clear that Rhine had instigated the circumstances so that the meeting would occur. As Slocum realized the duplicity of the man, not to mention his skill and, above all, his tenacity, he was aware of his own admiration. He'd met a number of manipulators in his life, but none could make a scratch on Bark Rhine. As these thoughts now invaded him he found that he was grinning. Grinning because he realized what he was up against—a man who had the slipperiness of a coyote, the honor of a snake in the grass. Indeed, Slocum told himself that he was relieved; relieved to at last discover that the whole situation with Otis, Jake Whistler, and Ridey Bones was beginning to fit like the pieces of a puzzle into an all-encompassing frame.

Plain as a pikestaff he could see now that Bark Rhine was a man who let others make their own decisions, and some of those later discovered that the decision they had made was the one that Bark Rhine had aimed for in the first place.

It was just then that Slocum realized somebody was close on his back trail.

He kicked his horse into a brisk canter, rounding a stand of cottonwood trees as the trail rose and narrowed. Then he began searching for a place where he could break off into the trees and circle back without leaving any sign.

At last he came upon the spot he was looking for, a narrow, almost invisible trail that led into the trees. Instantly he kneed the Appaloosa in that direction.

The trail wound up through the cottonwoods and then some pine and fir, making a semicircle so that he came out on a ledge that gave him a clear view of his back trail. The section the riders would be reaching in a moment was almost directly below him now, and he was fully protected by tall pine and fir.

They were coming fast now, two riders, and quickly he drew the Winchester from its saddle scabbard. Rhine had given it to him as a sign of good faith. Directly below him, the area on which he was aiming his sight, the trail narrowed, so that the riders would have to go single file.

And suddenly they were both in full sight.

"Pull up!" His words cracked down on the two men like a pair of bullets. And there was no question of them hearing him. Furiously they drew rein, tugging at their horses's mouths in their anger at being thrown down on so unsuspectingly.

Cursing, red-faced, one of them slashing his reins at his horse in frustration, they pulled up.

"What's your hurry, boys?" Slocum dismounted and now stood just above them at the edge of the big rock, with a stand of trees and bilberry bushes behind him.

"Don't figure you can outdraw me," he snapped as one of the pair made an abortive move toward his handgun.

"You got us mixed up with somebody else, mister," the other of the pair said. "We got nothing you could want."

"I want to know where you're hustling to so fast," Slocum said, his words cold.

"Just heading back to the Circle BR. We got work to do for a livin'. What in hell you want with us?"

"I just told you," Slocum said, his voice like ice. "I want to know where you're heading. Or were you just interested in where I might be heading?"

"We don't even know you, mister."

"You do now. I want to know why your boss told you to follow my trail."

"Nobody told us," said the heavier of the pair, a man with a thick mustache and flashing dark eyes.

His companion sniffed, his eyes darting to the handgun at Slocum's waist.

"I believe I just saw the both of you at the Circle BR, which happens to be in the other direction from where you pair said you were heading."

Nobody gave answer to that.

Then, the shorter of the pair spoke. "Mister, we be

minding our own business, that's all. No point for you to throw down on us. We done nothing to you; don't even know you. Neither of us even knows your name or what you're doing here on Circle BR range."

"Never set eye on you before," said his companion, mumbling the words in a sulky way.

Slocum spat easily, moved his head slightly, and reached up with his left hand and readjusted his Stetson hat to shade his eyes better from the brilliant sun. A part of him was listening for the possibility of the pair on the trail below him not being alone.

"You two are from the bunch I saw up at the Circle BR," he repeated.

"How can you tell that, mister?" asked the taller of the pair.

"I can smell you. You both got the same stink as those others."

He squinted at the sun, measuring the time of day by its place in the sky and then squinted at his captives. "You unbuckle everything, especially anything you might be hiding and figuring to use later. And just remember, you'll be less trouble to yours truly here dead than alive."

They regarded him solemnly then, and in a jiffy had unbuckled their gunbelts and dropped all their weapons on the ground.

"Now you can head back the way you came."

"Listen, mister . . ."

Slocum simply moved the barrel of the Winchester ever so slightly.

One of the horses snorted, rolled his eyes and threw down his head to bite a tick on his chest.

"Git!"

Sneering, but not daring to go any further they turned their horses and walked them fast down the trail.

Slocum didn't move. He sat listening, as still as the

rock that was all around him. Once again he realized the kind of man he was up against. Bark Rhine was all kinds of things, that was clear; in particular he was a man who did things differently.

Right now, Slocum was swept by the need to get to Ridey Bones and his wife and granddaughter. And fast.

He had just passed the big butte, not far from where he'd braced the two Circle BR riders when he spotted the cloud of dust. Drawing rein, he sat his horse, studying it. At first the dust cloud was just a spot on the horizon, but as he watched it come nearer he saw it was long and narrow, rising out of the sunbaked earth, enveloping everything under it. And it was now coming toward Slocum with a rumbling roar.

The crack of a rifle suddenly cut the air, and then came another, and still another. The cloud of dust seemed to explode into a hundred parts, swiftly coming together again in a huge mass. Slocum thought of an avalanche. He dug his heels deep in the flanks of his horse, and the Appaloosa leaped forward like any top cow pony to meet the oncoming mass of charging beef.

For by now Slocum had seen that they were cattle, stampeding with a sudden terror, their thundering hooves making the earth tremble and roar like a great drum. He rode straight for the center of the stampede. His cow pony was well broken, turning quickly when the leaders were reached, slowing down its pace to stay just about a jump or two ahead of them, allowing Slocum to lash their faces with the honda knot on the end of his lariat rope.

The blows made the leaders turn just enough to change their course; in moments they had turned completely around, and the other cattle followed and soon formed into a huge milling mass.

The swing riders of the herd, who had been unable to reach the leaders, now surrounded the cattle, keeping them milling about until suddenly the stampede was over and the beeves were grazing peacefully as though nothing at all had happened.

Suddenly Ridey Bones appeared on a big sorrel gelding.

"By God, that's about the neatest trick of turning back a stampede these here eyes have ever seen. And by God right in the nick of time," he went on, his face reddening as his voice grew louder. "When I get a hold of them sonsofbitches who started that little party, I am gonna shoot their balls off!"

He was rigid with fury, his face copper-colored as he swore, spat, glared, and fussed with his horse.

"By God, if I'd the money I'd hire you for my ramrod right now!" he declared.

Slocum grinned at him. "Done."

"Eh? What'd you say?"

"I said 'Done'. You want a ramrod, you got one, mister."

"Well I'll be whang-danged! Yahoooo!" And the old boy let go a cowboy yell and beamed with surprise and goodwill on his new foreman.

Ridey Bones had two men helping with the herd, which had been stampeded by horsemen no one recognized. It didn't take all that long for Slocum, Ridey, and the two extra hands to bunch the stock and move them to another part of the range.

"You two stay on guard this night," Ridey said, "till twelve. Then me and Slocum here will relieve you."

The men nodded and rode off.

"Would have been better for you an' me to split up,

Ridey, but I know you had some reason for doing it this way, letting them two work together."

"I got a reason," the old man said.

"Like you want to find out who started the stampede."

"Who do you think did?" Ridey asked.

"I figure same as you," said Slocum. "Them two. They have got to be in on it. But who are they working for? Is it Rhine?"

"You can triple your bet on that one," the old man said sourly.

"It's more of his pressure then. Like the three that rode in and tried to set you up with a shootout."

"It's been going on a spell. One of these days I'll just have to ride on over to the sonofabitch's outfit and bullet the shit out of him."

"That will be just what he wants," Slocum pointed out sourly.

"To get his ass shot off?"

"No. He wants you to lose your temper and that's when you'll lose your ass, is what I am telling you." He looked at his companion quietly for a moment. "Figure it out. They're taking their time, they're aiming to wear you down. You don't tell me this is the first time something like this has happened. Or those three saddle tramps riding in the other day and playing tough with you. You can expect more. You know that same as I do."

The old man was nodding. "I know. That's what I for sure know."

"They'll wear you down," Slocum said. "Look, I know you're one tough hombre, but they'll keep after you. Whoever's behind this has a lot of patience and he'll just keep going at it and going at it."

"Jesus!"

"I want to know why," Slocum said.

"So do I."

Slocum was looking at him steadily. "I think you know why, my friend."

Ridey looked at him with surprise all over his face. "I ain't got a notion . . ." he began to say.

But Slocum cut him off. "Bullshit! You know damn well what he's after! So stop pretending! You know damn well, and you better face up to it now by God. Better now than later."

"I dunno. I got no notion . . ."

"Look," Slocum said, and he stood facing the man squarely. They dismounted in the horse corral right outside the barn. Slocum took a moment to feel the weather. "It could be fixin' to storm some."

Ridey let fly a thick jet of saliva and reaching down scratched deep into his crotch. "I can tell the weather pretty good for an old party," he declared with a note of triumph.

"You better be telling what you figure Rhine's boys'll be up to next," Slocum said. "But what I want to know is what they're after."

Ridey spat again, this time swiftly and with obvious irritation. "Shit, how many times I got to tell ya? He is after this section of range. Anybody with half an eye can figger that."

"And anybody with a whole eye can figger something different," Slocum said. And he took out his makings and began building a smoke.

Ridey watched him. "You got some fly up yer ass, I can tell. You ain't satisfied with what I tell you. If you were a full-time cattle pusher then you'd likely agree with me. I cannot see any other reason for that sonofabitch Rhine wantin' to gobble up all this here land."

"Can you see any reason why Otis is expected in this country?" Slocum asked, and he looked at the older man with a face that only a poker player would have appreciated.

The old man studied it for a minute and then he said, "Shit. Forgot about that sonofabitch. Shit."

"Forget Otis and you can forget your ass," Slocum said.

"I mean I forgot for the minute," Ridey said. "That sonofabitch is a man hard to get out of your mind."

"That's the point," Slocum said. "He's a man who'll keep us sharp like we need to be. And I want to know all you can tell me about him. And about Jake Whistler," he added with emphasis.

A silence fell then, with Ridey Bones searching around his teeth for some stray flecks of tobacco, and with some scratching about in his arms and crotch, and once at the back of his neck. "Can't help you much there," he said finally. "Only run into Otis a few times; and Whistler even hardly that much."

Slocum was standing swing-hipped in front of him now, and he straightened up as he said, "I think it's about time you came clean with me."

The old man glared at him.

"Could be you didn't know Otis more than a bit," Slocum said. "But one'll get you two quicker'n a cat can lick his own ass that you knew Mr. Jake Whistler a whole helluva lot more than a bit." And he lifted his Stetson hat off his head just slightly and readjusted it with the brim further over his face. Then he stood swing-hipped with his thumbs hooked in his gunbelt as he squinted at Ridey Bones, hard, without a muscle moving in his face, or maybe anywhere else.

A long sigh slid all the way down through Ridey's bony frame, ending with a long sniff as he reached up and rubbed the end of his nose.

"Reckon . . ." The word was hardly audible as he

looked out across the wide valley.

Except that Slocum could tell the old boy was also looking at something else; something more important to him than those big snowcapped mountains.

Slocum waited. His own eyes caught the arc of an eagle high in the light blue sky. The day was suddenly cool on his hands and face and now the light was moving quickly out of the sky. Across the wide valley the sun was still glistening on the snowcaps that covered the great shoulders of the Absarokas.

Ridey suddenly started to speak.

" 'Course there wasn't no law about in those days. Which allowed for a bit of fun an' frolic. Finality was wide open, more cow camp than town, though there was a saloon and a cathouse after awhile. But the boys had it all their way. I remember the time I first seen Jake Whistler." He paused to spit at a rock, hitting it plumb center, Slocum noted with amusement. And Ridey looked at him a bit cockeyed for his noticing.

"By God," he said. "You mind a feller tightern' a bull's ass in fly-time, don'cha."

"Place was like a roost, was it?"

Ridey nodded. "Where Whistler and his boys hung out. Them days there was a few cabins, a saloon, girls. Though it started out more simple. Then, 'course with the gang bein' so handy with what they were doin'—trains, the stage, now and again a bank— things improved. Gang got bigger, though Jake, he didn't believe in havin' too many men about. Too easy for someone to run his mouth, he used to say. But by God that man knew how to run an outfit. And, mind you, he never took anything from anybody who couldn't handle a loss. I mean such as the railroad, the banks, the stage company. He never bothered regular people. I say this, by God: Jake Whistler was a good man. He just happened to work the other side of the law. And if you been around enough of them lawmen like I been, then you know that most of them ain't worth a bucket of shit. Less, by God!" And he spat vigorously into a clump of sage that he'd been aiming at for some time as he'd been speaking, and now hit plumb center.

Slocum said nothing to all of this. He just sniffed, spat, ran the palm of his hand alongside his jaw, and squinted at the weather.

Ridey said, "So, I knew him. Might as well admit it. I can say it to you, I do believe. If I can't, then at my age what the hell it matters I dunno." And he nodded a couple of times, as if in agreement with himself.

"That still don't explain why this feller Otis . . ."

"Otis was part of the gang," Ridey cut in. "Let me tell you right off he was a no-good sonofabitch . . . and I mean son-of-a-bitch!"

He fell silent for a moment, and Slocum let him ruminate. He was plenty glad the old boy was opening up.

"Somethin' happened 'tween Whistler and Otis, I'd wager to say," Slocum put in after a long enough silence for Ridey to turn some more of it over.

The old man nodded. "Easy enough to figger. Lookin' back of course." He sniffed, took a half step forward and leaning over, blew his nose between his thumb and forefinger. Followed by a clearing of his throat. And in a moment Slocum saw that Ridey Bones was older than he'd first figured.

"A man could of augured what was goin' to happen," he said, his eyes turning back again to the past.

"Otis got uppity."

"Otis took to bein' real damn uppity. An' 'course anybody with half the sense of a pissant could have figgered it. But I saw that Jake was just playin' his rope, letting Otis hang himself. Which he sure enough did."

"Otis wasn't so smart then," Slocum said, simply by way of encouraging more talk.

"He was a stupid shit." Ridey paused to let fly again, this time at a clump of cow dung. "But Jake, he minded his time and sure enough Otis stuck his foot in it. See, there was always people hanging around Whistler. Men, I am talking about. 'Course women too. The women liked Jake and he liked the women. But men also hung about, and kids. Somethin' about the man . . ." His eye turned suddenly on Slocum, sort of sideways, Slocum thought, and then he said, "Puts me in mind of yourself, mister." And he paused, chewing swiftly, like he was trying to catch up with his thoughts. "Anyways, there was a kid who used to hang about. Dunno who he was exactly, except I'd heard he was more'n half Injun, and Whistler sort of took him on after whoever his father was got killed. I dunno the whole of it, but it was like that. Kids hung around Jake. But don't get me wrong. Jake Whistler was no easy mark, he was no one to run around with a bible in his pocket. He was . . . well, I guess he was just what he was—himself. An' this kid he was about a good bit of the time, helping out with chores and the like and kinda liking to be around Jake who for his part didn't treat him like a kid, even though he couldn't have been more'n maybe twelve, thirteen. Jake treated him like he was one of the men. I mean, just about, exceptin' for the drinkin' and girls and like that. Well, one time in the Double Deck Saloon Otis seen the kid there and started in on how he wanted to know why this kid was always there with the men, especially bein' a damn Injun. And by God, 'fore a man could scratch his balls there Otis was lyin' flat on his back on the floor with the blood running all over his ugly face. Then

Jake Whistler ordered him to get up on his feet and haul ass the hell out of there and never show hisself again."

He stopped, scratching deep into one armpit.

"I have heard that Otis dry-gulched him," Slocum said.

"That is correct."

"But what's he doing back here in Finality Gulch, is what I am wanting to know." And he was wondering too what Heavy Hank Finnegan had to do with Otis and Finality Gulch, and why he himself was right here and now on the scene.

"I dunno. I got no idea how come Otis is here. If he is. I ain't seen him yet. I heard he was about, somewhere in the country, but I ain't seen him." He spat suddenly and swiftly. "And I don't 'specially want to." Ridey cocked his head, closing one eye to regard Slocum with a special intention. "You figger Otis was in on this stampede?"

"I don't know. But according to my reckoning, he should be around this part of the country by now. And I wouldn't be surprised if he was working for Rhine."

"It was Rhine who done this, the stampede," Ridey said, nodding his head. " 'Course he could have got Otis in on it. But besides that, what's he want Otis for anyways? He's out to run me off of my spread, which he ain't going to do long as I got breath in my body, but he don't need somebody like Otis for that. And I'll be damned if I can figger why he's so goddam eager to get my range. He doesn't need it all that bad."

Slocum was squinting at the sky.

"You catching something?" Ridey asked after a stretch of silence.

"I am wondering just what Rhine would want a man like Otis for. He sure doesn't need the likes of Otis for wrangling you off your spread. Hell, gunmen kind of grow on trees in this part of the country."

"They sure as hell do." And the old man nodded vigorously, sucking his teeth and scratching himself, all at the same time.

"Then," said Slocum. "There has got to be something else."

Ridey Bones was staring at him. "Like how you mean that? Like what else? There ain't no gold that anybody knows about. There ain't anything anybody'd want to spend his time at. So what is it?"

Slocum watched him, feeling him as he spoke vigorously, wagging his old head a little, and finally spitting a copious stream of brown and yellow tobacco in the direction of some horse droppings.

Slocum waited, knowing that the old man was wrestling with something. Something from the past? About Jake Whistler and his gang? He had not forgotten what Heavy Hank Finnegan had hinted, or actually said for that matter, about loot. At the time he had taken it as a throwaway, thinking that Finnegan had spoken of bandit loot to steer him away from something else. Only what? And for a moment he considered confronting Ridey Bones with the question of a cache hidden by Whistler years ago, and that maybe that was the reason for Otis's return to Finality Gulch after so many years. Even the reason for his escape, as Finnegan had hinted.

But he could see that Ridey was fighting it. Fighting something, at any rate. And he realized too that he could be wrong. He was pretty sure now that it was not the moment to push the old man. He'd gotten a good bit already. Now he had to let it cook a little and see what he came up with in the next day or two. Or see what would take place. He had the feeling of something inevitable happening. At the same time, he knew it was not the moment to push Ridey Bones.

Then, as if in answer to his inner questioning, the old man said, "Weather fixin' to change some, smells like. Come on over to the outfit and put down yer duffel. We'll git Janey to cook us up some supper."

10

"I like it here. I like the mountains, the land, the great sky. I love the smell of the horses, and the cattle too, and the firewood when it's just been chopped."

"And the people?" Slocum asked. "You like them, at least from what I see of the way you are with your grandparents."

She nodded. From the corner of his eye he caught the movement of her head, as the sun disappeared behind the high rimrocks across the great valley spreading below them. They were sitting at the top of a draw that cut up into a stand of spruce and pine, a good way above the ranch house. Slocum watched the thin string of smoke coming from the kitchen smoke-stack, as he pondered the exchange he'd had earlier with Ridey Bones in connection with the girl sitting beside him on the saddle blanket. For he had wondered about Janey being about at such a time; a visitor, even though a relative, but green to the country and its ways. He wasn't so sure that a man like Otis or Bark Rhine might not make a move in the girl's direction. He wouldn't put anything past either of the pair. A good way to get at Ridey Bones, through his granddaughter.

And he was sure it would be a way that a man such as Bark Rhine wouldn't overlook.

It was a special evening, the sky washed with stars and stardust too, with the great globe of the moon at its most magnificent. Slocum often wondered about the distance of that starry world from the earth, and the size of a man in comparison to all that he was looking at—and feeling—right now.

And then—it seemed as sudden, silent, and instant as their breathing—they were in each other's arms. His mouth found hers as her tongue sank deep into him. He could feel her quivering with her passion and his erection was about to rip through his pants. She had her hand on it, rubbing, squeezing, and then she was unbuttoning him. He, meanwhile, had reached into her blouse and found the hard knob of her nipple. His hand felt it get harder as he also explored the silky skin of her breast.

Now she had his erection out of his pants. It was quite a struggle for it was pinning him into his clothes, but she finally gave it a pull and it sprang into the evening air. In the next instant she was down on him, his cock plunging halfway down her throat.

Meanwhile, he had reached down and unbuttoned her riding pants and pulled them down, his hand feeling her soft, but supremely eager buttocks as they began rubbing and thrusting at each other—she at his great erection, and he at her soaking bush.

"I want you, I want you!" She gasped the words as her buttocks, lying on the blanket as she received his driving cock, pumped up and down in unison with him. Her hands clutched his thighs, his buttocks, and now reaching down she squeezed his balls. Slocum thought he would come right then, but he managed to delay it into a further exquisite tension and she began to pump more swiftly on his great pole. Faster and faster they rode each other, gasping, stifling screams of joy as they rode together in ultimate ecstasy to the end of the known world. Exploding at the exact same instant in a wave of come, their buttocks thrashing together, their lips sucking and tearing as each drove a tongue deep into the other's eager mouth, and she spread even wider while he rode harder and higher and faster and faster still, until there was nothing else. There was no time, no gesture, no immediate recognition of a touch, a movement, a feeling . . . they shared a brief moment that was both unendurable and without time.

They lay gasping in each other's arms and legs, soaking wet from the climax of their separate, yet for that unendurable split second, identical lives.

They slept.

How long they slept he didn't know, but he had the sense of it being reasonably short. And good enough, for he had no wish to have somebody slipping up on them at such a moment. In short, as he told himself with more than a touch of wryness, he had no wish to be caught with his pants down.

They awakened as easily as they'd fallen asleep, and just as happy, with her snuggling against him and he with his arm around her. But not for long. He had heard something. Had heard it while he still slept.

He reached over, gently touching one hand to her lips, and putting his other hand on his six gun. He felt her coming awake under his fingers, and he squeezed her cheek a couple of times to caution her. Then he was up on his feet, crouching as he moved further into the trees.

He had signaled her to stay where she was, to stay motionless, counting on her to understand the pressure of his fingers and hand. Now, from inside the ring of brush he saw that she was still there. And making no sound.

Then he heard the horses, a whiffle, the creaking of leather, the jangle of a bit. He judged it to be a pair. Likely outriders, come for a look-see at the Bones' herd, which right now was under the surveillance of Ridey Bones and his two hired hands, Cal Tillary and Homer Holmes. Slocum had pulled an earlier watch on his own, due to the fact that Homer's horse had thrown a shoe and Ridey insisted on shoeing him before putting the rider on duty. At any rate, it had been the early evening when Slocum had insisted on taking the watch alone, for he wanted to see if either of the two hired hands would somehow reveal whether or not they might be working secretly for Bark Rhine. He believed that changing a man's schedule, setting him up in fresh, unexpected circumstances could, and sometimes truly did, give enough surprise and unusual framework where something could turn up.

In other words, he had told Ridey that he had better check on his own men. Bark Rhine was going to stop at nothing in order to get whatever it was he wanted, and he wasn't going to hire any half-assed cowpokes or saddle bums without figuring how he could use them.

"It's a rare man can't be reached," Slocum had told Ridey. "Give a feller enough rope and more than likely he'll hang himself. Give him enough booty and he'll turn on you. You can't trust trail hands you've just picked up like them two. You got to know a man a good while and see him in action 'fore you can trust your life with him."

"That's what I know," Ridey had warmly agreed. "But sometimes a man don't have the time to check—like those two saddle bums I took on."

"Don't get me wrong," Slocum had told him. "The pair of them might turn out good as gold. But a man's got to know it inside. I don't trust 'em, but I don't not trust them. You get me?"

"I do. Now, mister you have driven that nail; there is no need to countersink it."

To which Slocum had responded with a guffaw of laughter. That old boy was a rich one, there was no denying it!

Now, listening as he waited in the stand of cottonwoods, he knew his own caution had been damn close, if not right on the mark.

Someone was moving through the trees and brush, not very far from where he was standing. He was certain it was one man, but at the same time he was damned sure that if it were one of Bark Rhine's men he would certainly not be alone.

Slocum stood absolutely still, listening. He couldn't hear the girl, and he was surprised and pleased at her response to his caution. She wasn't making a sound; usually an impossible condition for a greener new to the country.

Now he heard the man closer to where he was standing. He was off the thin trail himself, protected by brush, and also helped by the fact that he knew of the other man's presence. At the same time he was pretty sure the intruder was not yet aware of himself or the girl.

Then he heard another branch crack, telling him exactly where the man was. He was about to make his move, but something stopped him. Something about the sound of that branch breaking was too obvious. Clearly the man he was listening to wanted to be heard. It was an old trick, decoying an enemy into responding to the sound, thus giving his position away to a third party. An old Indian trick, the difference being that an Indian could pull it off better. Slocum was not fooled, and so he remained as he was: standing, slightly crouched, and absolutely still, though not rigid. Not a single muscle in his body was tight as he waited, feeling and listening for the man in the trees as well as listening to himself.

He waited.

When it finally came, it wasn't a sound, but a smell. And he was relieved, for he'd known that somebody was very close, indeed, very, very close. Yet, he did not feel free to make a move. For it could so easily be a trap so that he would give himself away.

No, it didn't come to his ear, but to his nose. He smelled the man. And he knew that much more than likely he was dealing with at least one hide hunter or buffalo skinner. A bunch that was famous not for their intelligence so much as their smell. The hide hunter did not believe in washing himself too strenuously. Indeed, he smelled exactly like what he was: a member of the buffalo-hunting, buffalo-skinning fraternity.

And he knew it was not an Indian. No self-respecting Sioux or Cheyenne or Arapaho would make that much noise, nor emit that particular smell. So there were at least two. They would of course be working in pairs. The problem was the girl. If either of them discovered her, God knows what would happen.

Slocum stood very still, the only movement being his breathing and the circulation of his blood. And in that stillness he came together in a new way—relaxed, yet at the same time with a tension like a bow ready to release its arrow. It was the second man he was concerned with. Where was he?

Well, there was a way to find out. He was pretty sure that he could assume the man near him would be facing the clearing, and more than likely lining up roughly with the girl. The point would be to catch his attention. He grinned at the thought. Indeed, he often grinned at such thoughts which were so obvious that you had to discover them for yourself over and over again. For indeed everything was a question of attention. Take a gunfighter: one split second of lost attention could, and usually did, lose him his life. The same when it came to riding a bronc, wrestling a roped calf, or bulldogging a steer.

Then he heard it. It was almost a breath. In fact, it was breath in the form of a muffled belch. And Slocum smelled the booze.

Now he was even more still, more silent, and it seemed that not even time was moving through his body. At the same time he was easing himself toward the man. Moving with the silence of a shadow, he managed to get even closer to the source of the smell. He hoped that the man in front of him would be so caught up with the agitation in his stomach, and with enough inner noise, that his timing would surely be off, and he wouldn't be so apt to notice an unexpected visitor.

Carefully, Slocum moved through the brush, the trees, the bushes, feeling his way with each step and moving with the soft silence of shadow.

Then all at once he was almost on top of his quarry. To his surprise, the two men were very close together, which made it more difficult for him. His aim of course was to knock out one and then turn swiftly on the second man. But there would of necessity be that time lapse between the two, when the second man would be alerted. There was nothing he could do about that; except possibly a trick he had learned from some Shoshone braves a few years back. The trick was to make one man think that his companion was one of the enemy.

In only a moment or two Slocum had approached the man nearest him, at a point where his companion was not more than a few feet away. This was the bigger of the two men, he could tell now in the filtered moonlight coming through the trees.

In the next second or two he had taken two quick

steps toward the bigger man, and smashed him in the back of the neck with his Colt .44. The man fell as though poleaxed. His falling body landed with a thump and Slocum knew the other man had heard.

"Red! That you, Red? Red . . ."

Slocum stood stock still, as the other man approached. Crouched low, he felt rather than actually saw the man coming, and now he could hear him. For he was making little effort to be all that quiet. His partner's silence had clearly alarmed him.

"Red? You there . . . ?"

And Slocum rose behind him and brought his Colt smashing down on the back of the man's neck. There were now two unconscious bodies lying across the narrow deer trail.

Swiftly, Slocum took the precaution of removing their weapons, and hurried back to where Janey was waiting for him.

"We'd better get going fast," he said.

The girl was ready, and in almost the next breath they had rolled their blanket and were on their way back to the ranch. As he started off with the girl he knew it had been good work.

But he knew too that shortly the pair would be missed, and more than likely backup support would be on its way.

As he approached the ranch houses with Janey he reached over and took her hand. Her fingers gripped his.

"John, those men . . . Who were they?"

"I don't know. All I can say is they were up to no good."

She gave a short laugh at that. "But they were dangerous, weren't they? I had a feeling they were."

"They were dangerous," he said, and he squeezed her hand gently.

By now they were almost at the door of the house and she turned to him and said, "What will happen now? John, I have a feeling—such a strong feeling—that something bad is going to happen."

"I do believe you're right," he said. "And so we'll all have to keep really alert. I want you to stay in your house as much as possible."

"But isn't there something I can do in the way of helping?"

He shook his head. He was standing in front of her now, looking down into her face. The early moonlight made it possible for them to see each other clearly. "Janey, the best thing you can do is keep alert and make sure that your grandmother is all right. I've a notion she needs you right now. And for that matter, your grandpa too. They're both old, and you can help them. Best way for that is to stay low and stay indoors. Your grandfather won't listen to you, but your grandma, while she looks to me to be the kind who does her own thinking, she could probably do a little leaning on you about now."

They were right next to the house now, and he touched the sleeve of her blouse only very lightly, though she must have felt it.

He was about to say something more, but she spoke first.

"John, I want to tell you something."

"I'm listening."

Again the moon was behind a cloud, and, as always, he felt the change in the earth.

When she didn't speak right away, he wanted to say something, he wanted to draw her out. He felt something mysterious about this girl, and he wanted to find out who she truly was. Yes, it was as though she was holding something back from him. Only what?

When the silence lengthened, he thought he should

speak, but decided to wait. It was obvious to him that she had something heavy on her mind.

She took a step closer to him, for as they'd approached the cabin they had moved slightly apart, just in case either of the Bones might have been at a window. But now she stood quite close, though he knew she wasn't looking for an embrace, but rather had something to say.

"John, there's something I want to tell you," she repeated.

He looked down at her, for she was some inches shorter. "Yes, I know," he said.

"You know! Oh, I see, you mean you feel I have something to say, but what it is, that's something else."

"I'd say it's both."

She stared at him in surprise.

"I'd say you were wanting to tell me that Ridey and Millie ain't your grandpa and grandma after all. But that maybe you're wondering who is."

Her mouth had dropped, her eyes stared at him. She looked as though she was about to laugh in surprise, then cry in anguish. She did neither. She stood there staring at him.

"I know they're not your grandparents," he said.

The fingers on her right hand were suddenly touching the side of her face, as her lips fell apart and her eyes stared at him with total astonishment.

"How on earth did you ever know that? I can't imagine . . . I can't . . ."

"You don't look anywhere near like either of them," Slocum said.

"But . . ."

"I could say I guessed it."

"But . . ."

"Did Ridey tell you to pretend you were his granddaughter? That it would be safer for you here?"

She nodded, still with an expression of disbelief in her whole manner.

"Safer from what?"

"I—I don't know. But from the way the two of them spoke I just assumed it was because of the rough way things are out here, especially for women it seems. And they—or at least Ridey—said there were a lot of bad people around, and that if I was going to be asking around, and searching for my father, it would be better if I had some sort of family or home, some place settled so there wouldn't be any awkward questions that I couldn't answer."

"And you've no notion who your dad was? That it?"

She nodded. "I don't. I don't ever remember seeing him even. All I know from my mother is that he decided one day to come out West and make his stake, as they say, and that then he would send for us. Except, he never did. So I have simply come looking."

"Can you tell me what his name is?"

"His name was Jake Sturgis."

Slocum said nothing; he simply squinted at her.

"I wondered if maybe he'd gotten into some kind of trouble out here and had changed his name. All I want is to find out if he's alive or dead. And if I could see him maybe, just once, and talk to him." She nodded, as though agreeing with what she'd just said, and in fact agreeing with how she felt about the whole thing. "You know the name?" she asked.

And Slocum was struck by her tone of voice; for it was clear that she had no expectation that he would know it.

"Sturgis? Never heard the name," Slocum said. He stood quietly looking down into her face. "I'd like to help you look, though I wouldn't know where to start even."

She looked up at him, and he saw the tears in her eyes.

"As far as I'm concerned, you've already started," she said.

11

One of Bark Rhine's favorite pastimes was practicing the techniques of his original trade, which he had learned on the Mississippi some years ago—and, of course, under a different name. That is to say, he enjoyed a game of cards, dice, and other forms of gambling. In fact, he saw his whole way of life as a distinct gamble. For the gambling wasn't only in cards, but in the betting, and not only against opponents, but often with oneself. Although Mr. Rhine greatly enjoyed card and dice playing and betting in general, his main interest was in the practice of his advantage tools.

And yet, he no longer actually used such tools as the holdout, the shaved deck, readers, or loaded dice. He believed that in order to be sharp in a business deal, a man certainly had to know all the angles of honest as well as dishonest gambling. The point being, he was fond of telling himself, to know a crook you had to be able to think like a crook. Bark Rhine prided himself on being good at that. He could spot a fourflusher the minute he set foot in the gaming room, or indeed anywhere else.

And so on certain occasions Mr. Rhine put aside

his solitude, his anonymity as far as society was concerned, and took pleasure in venturing forth into the heated atmosphere of the gaming tables, even rubbing shoulders with the regular folk and clientele of such dens of iniquity. On the other hand, he was not above, or beneath attending gambling sessions in such highfaluting institutions as the notable Cheyenne Club, frequented by the cream of the Stockmen's Association, or at other moments, indulging his penchant for frolic at such noble institutions as Annie Chambers' Fabulous House of Fantastic Pleasure in Kansas City. Indeed, Bark Rhine saw himself as a man for any walk of life who could and did pick and choose to do exactly as he wished. In his day he had run everything—from the humble shell game to the famous and very special Western Shuffle.

But best of all, he enjoyed relating and at the same time instructing his closest companion on some of his skills and adventures; he used her as a sounding board for future or even present endeavors in his pursuit of whatever it was he was after at the moment. For example, his recent adventure in salting part of the New Mexico desert with diamonds and then selling shares in the "Ajax Diamond Research Company," with its eastern Board of Directors, all of course under the invisible hand of Bark Rhine. He'd pulled that one off like a whisper. Cleaned up! And not the slightest shadow of suspicion even breathed in his direction.

Right now, he was chatting with his paramour as they lay in naked satiation after one of their powerful sexual assaults on one another. They lay in the wide double bed in the room next to his office in the big ranch house overlooking the valley.

"Catherine," he was whispering in her ear. "Catherine, wake up!"

And all at once she sat bolt upright, her large boobs

hitting him in the face as he broke into joyous laughter.

"Boo-boo, what's the matter?"

"Nothing, my dear. Why do you ask," he said, wiping the tears of laughter from his eyes.

"Because you never—never—have called me by my name! Do you realize that? And suddenly now you call me Catherine. I can only feel that something's the matter, something is troubling you." She leaned closer to him. "Wasn't it . . . satisfactory, my dear?"

"My God, how can you ask? IT was a total delight! And I do realize that—and you're absolutely correct! I have never called you by your first name. But now I have!"

At this they both broke into raucous laughter.

"Boo-boo, is the door locked?"

"It is. And my dear, don't always be worrying about that. For the life of me, I can't decide whether you want the door to be locked or unlocked when we have our fun!"

To his utter astonishment, her cheeks reddened slightly and then a full blush swept her. He felt a thrill run through him. What a delight she was!

"I'll try it, my dear."

And he sat up, swung his feet to the floor and walked over to the door and tried it.

"Locked it is!"

Her eyes were shining as he came back to bed. "I believe we got interrupted when you were telling me about the game you were taking part in the other night."

"Indeed we were," he said, smiling down at her as she lay on her back with her knees up. "But actually, my dear I was telling you—perhaps I should say, instructing you—in the art of card playing. A special shuffle, as it were. In fact, it is known as the Western Shuffle, but alas, you weren't really listening, my dear." He sighed, grinning lecherously at her until she burst again into laughter.

"Boo-boo, I believe you weren't satisfied—you want to do it again," and she spread her legs wide open and beckoned him to mount her.

He was chuckling now, joining her, but his tool was not as hard as it had been. "I want him to rest a minute, my dear. After all, we've done it twice this evening."

"I am perfectly happy to wait until that thing gets as big as . . . as . . . as what?"

"How about a flagpole?" he said grinning, feeling the stirring between his legs.

There came a sudden knock at the door.

"Damn it," he said. And then called out, "What is it?"

"It's Myles, Mr. Rhine. I have news from the men you sent over to the Greybull this morning. Are you ready for it now?"

He rose, crossed to the door, and put his hand on the knob, but he didn't open it.

"I am busy right now. Tell me through the door, unless there's someone around who can hear you."

He could hear the man on the other side clearing his throat. "Nobody here, except myself."

"Shoot."

"They got beat up. Hines and Fiddler. By that feller Slocum."

He stood silently, taking in that news, his hand still on the doorknob, while the girl, sitting up in bed, watched him.

"They are still amongst the living are they?"

There followed a moment of silence from the other side of the door, and at last the man said, "Didn't catch ya there, Mister Rhine."

"I said are the men still alive?"

"They are."

His voice was softer, as he half turned toward the girl on the bed. "What a pity."

A hard silence fell then. He watched her as she lay back. "How about Janey?" he said suddenly.

He watched her head lift as she looked at him. But she said nothing.

His voice lifted now as he called out, "Myles, I will see you later and you can give me a full report then."

"Will you want to see the men? Hines and Fiddler."

Mr. Rhine did not answer. He simply turned to the bed and walked toward it slowly, his eyes searching the naked body that lay there. Her eyes were closed. But he knew that she was not asleep.

The mattress gave under his weight as he sat down on the edge of the bed, but she didn't open her eyes.

Lifting his head, he looked toward the window. There was still light in the sky. His eyes swung back to the woman on the bed who still had her eyes closed.

Suddenly she opened her eyes and looked at him. But he could read no expression there.

"I was telling you about the Western Shuffle, my dear." He looked at her. Her eyes were again closed.

"My dear . . ."

"I'm listening."

"The game," he said, clearing his throat as his eyes lit up, "would be poker. And there have to be seven players for it to work. My dear, when it worked, it was simply beautiful!" He grinned and settled more of his weight on the bed, while she remained with her eyes closed.

"The dealer," he continued, "would call for a brand-new deck of cards. If an old deck was used he'd have to make sure that the cards were arranged in numerical order just as they are when they come from the factory—ace, deuce, trey, four, five, and so on up to the king." He cleared his throat and leaned more closely toward her for emphasis on what he was saying. "Because a new deck is supposed to be well mixed up before play begins, the dealer makes several false shuffles. He's fast, of course, and he's skilled at doing it. For instance, he lets all the cards in his right hand fall ahead of those in his left, or the other way around. It's actually no different than a straight cut except that the dealer pretends to shuffle the deck. You do it with your hands cupped." And he raised his hand to demonstrate. "Look."

Her eyes opened and she turned her head slightly to look at his hand.

"It's best to do it when the play is dull and others in the game are less observant."

He reached up and ran his fingers through his thinning hair. "Now then, after the fake shuffle and cut, the first round is dealt in the usual way from the top of the deck to all seven players. The next round, the same, except that the dealer takes the bottom card. On the third round the deal is again conventional to all seven players. The same on the fourth round, except the dealer takes his card from the bottom of the deck."

He paused again, letting it sink in. Her eyes were closed, but she murmured so that he would know she was listening.

"The critical round is the fifth. The first player on the dealer's immediate left gets the top card in order. Then, with his left thumb—he's holding the deck in his left hand—he slips back the top card far enough to allow him to deal the next card from under it, or the second card down." He paused. "Listen carefully, my dear."

A murmur came from her to indicate that she was listening.

"He repeats this maneuver twice more, and then to

the next man—he'll be the fifth player counting clockwise from the dealer—he slips the card that he's been holding back with his thumb. The sixth player—that's the man on the dealer's immediate right—gets his card in its regular order. That is, the card the sixth player gets is the same one he would have received anyway if the deal hadn't been disturbed." He was grinning at her as she continued to lie there with her eyes closed.

"The dealer now slips himself the bottom card, and so seven hands have been dealt."

He sat back, reaching for his glass, his eyes on the wall behind the bed, recalling every detail with perfect clarity.

"The first player—on the dealer's left—now has a pat full house and he'll make a good bet to protect his hand, but not big enough to scare the other players out of the game.

"The second, third, fourth, and fifth players will all have two pairs each, with an odd fifth card. This will be just enough to suck them in. The sixth player on the dealer's right will also have a full house and he will call the opening bet and raise.

"The dealer checks his hand. He has a pair and three other cards of one suit, and they are running consecutively, like the seven, eight and nine of hearts. He knows now that on the bottom of the deck there are the ten and jack of hearts that will give him a straight flush. But he doesn't bet; he calls, because he doesn't want to drive the others out of the game.

"The two pat full houses draw no cards, and that's to be expected, while the players holding two pairs do draw. However, it doesn't matter what they draw, because the four sets of two pairs can't be helped and they will drop out when the betting stiffens, leaving the dealer and the owners of the two full houses to fight it out.

"Now then, it gets interesting! The dealer's two cards from the bottom give him an unbeatable straight flush and he can bet it all the way. But he has got to bet conservatively until after the draw, on the very thin chance that somebody might demand a cut. He's also got to keep his eye on his last card, because if by chance it's a king or a queen he can't make a straight flush. Of course, this happens only about once in a dozen hands or more, in which case, if it did happen, he'd simply drop out, losing only his ante. If his last card is an ace, he's got to draw four cards, the deuce, trey, four, and five. But luckily, the ace shows up only about once in twenty deals."

He fell silent, reliving some of the earlier scenes in his life, from when he was a good deal younger, and the action had been fast and furious—and mostly on the hoof. Not like now, where he did his work in solitude, or from behind a desk, or through the agency of lieutenants and sublieutenants. Life in those earlier years had been more direct and, yes, more immediate, and, yes again, more exciting. Right now he felt a bit down.

He thought that she had fallen asleep and a stroke of irritation ran through him. Then, all at once and totally unexpectedly, her eyes opened and she lay there regarding him quietly.

His thoughts of the past slipped away to be replaced by his desire for her. She closed her eyes again and continued to lay there as she had been with her head squarely on the pillow. The sheet had fallen away from her and her bare breasts were exposed. Without opening her eyes she reached down and pulled the sheet up to cover herself. Suddenly he realized that she had been watching him from beneath her lowered eyelids, as he had sat there devouring her while his passion rose.

She pulled the sheet up to her chin.

"Catherine," he said. "Cathy. . . ."

She did not reply.

"Cathy. . . ." He reached out to touch her face and as he did so he felt the wetness on her cheek.

He felt suddenly as though he had been struck; he had never seen her cry. He drew his hand back. Yet she said nothing as the tears silently flowed from her eyes.

He continued to sit there watching her as the daylight began to die against the window, and shadow entered the bedroom. She lay there not moving, not speaking, as the tears flowed from her closed eyes and ran down her cheeks.

The room grew darker, but neither of them moved.

Bark Rhine sat on the edge of the bed, with his ankles crossed and with his hands in his lap. He was remembering how he used to run the shell game in the street outside Big Bill Mellody's saloon down in Waco, Texas. And later how he worked the riverboats on the Mississippi, and then the railroad hell on wheels. And then . . . and then. . . .

He looked down at her, only able to see the outline of her face, for it was almost dark now in the room.

And suddenly he heard himself saying her name, "Cathy . . . Cathy. . . ."

Her arms were tight around him as she drew him down.

"You bastard," she said. "Why did it take you so long. . . ."

Then he said, "I dunno what the hell you're talking about . . . I dunno . . ."

"That's part of it," she said in his ear, the words such a soft whisper that she alone heard them, and he did not.

• • •

At Tinker Crossing the big herd was restive. J. Parmelee and his crew had reached the small tributary of the Greybull that day and J. Parmelee had ordered a halt, figuring this to be a good place to bed down the herd. This order had not been received with joy by his hands. They had been following a long and very difficult drive north from Texas, and in the time-honored tradition of all trail herders, were at the bursting point to roar into town and drink and cavort with the booze and girls of Finality Gulch.

But J. Parmelee was not a man to be argued with, and he had his reasons for holding the herd at the crossing, reasons more than just to allow the beeves to rest and fatten on that good northern feed before driving them to the loading pens in Finality Gulch. He was just as eager as his men to hit town. But he had not counted on the message he'd received from the shipper, Fred Bass, that he should wait at the Crossing until met by Mr. Bark Rhine or his representative, who would explain the situation in Finality. J. Parmelee suspected the delay was simply because this was the first drive of Texas beef that Finality was receiving, so more than likely somebody had fucked up and not done the right thing such as seeing to the holding pens or some such bullshit. By God, there was always some goddamned delay at the end of a long drive. Damn people had no notion of what a man went through getting their goddamn beeves delivered so they could make their goddamn profit. There had also been the rumors of a quarantine about, all the way up from the Red River, which would mean he'd have to take the herd all the way round by Burksville, meaning more of a delay, and weight taken off all that beef on the hoof—meaning less money at the loading pens.

At the same time, he'd received word that no matter

what, he'd have to wait at Tinker Crossing no matter which way anything else went. And gradually, ever since he'd received that word down by Perry Butte, he'd had the notion that there was more afoot than those twenty-five hundred head of Texas beeves.

J. Parmelee—and nobody knew what the J. stood for—swung down from his best cow pony, the chunky little buckskin he'd broke himself just a year ago. It was now the best horse in his string, or so he considered. And J. Parmelee knew horses better than most—and cattle too, as a matter of fact.

He stood swing-hipped now in the early morning light under a somewhat windy sky listening to the bawling of the herd, a tin mug of coffee in one hand and two of cookie's fresh sourdough biscuits in the other.

"Looks to be fixin' to storm," Fletch, his trail boss, observed, stomping up in his high-heeled boots and yawning the sleep out of his red face. He stood on the other side of the saddle rig lying on the ground between them, right near the chuck wagon.

"Might." J. Parmelee squinted at the low sky, figuring the weather.

"Men're beginnin' to feel their oats," the foreman said.

"Figgers."

"How long you figger we'll wait here?"

"Till we get shut of our business with this feller what's comin'."

"Riders comin'," Fletch said.

"I heard."

"Sounds like a pair, maybe three."

"Two," J. Parmelee said, rubbing the side of his long, bony nose with his thumb. "Reckon it's our company." He took a bite of his sourdough biscuit.

He had just emptied his cup and dumped the grounds

onto a thick clump of sage when two horsemen rounded a small stand of box elders and pulled up, raising some dust, which was not appreciated by their host.

"You et?" J. Parmelee canted his head to one side as he spoke to the older of the men.

"If you have coffee that would be mighty agreeable," said the older man. "I take it you are Parmelee, I am Bark Rhine."

His companion, obviously a man of few words, simply nodded.

Meanwhile, Fletch had started back toward the chuck wagon, and Candy Myles, who had accompanied Bark Rhine followed close after him, leading his horse.

While waiting for the coffee, Bark Rhine had stepped down from his sorrel gelding, took out two cigars, and offered one to the cattleman. J. Parmelee accepted and slipped the Havana into his shirt pocket. "Take it later," he said and brought out his makings.

Bark Rhine had already bitten off the end of his cigar and was now lighting up.

"Got to travel mighty far to find a good smoke," he said genially.

"Sometimes you gotta do some travelin' to find a good woman," J. Parmelee said.

They walked over to where the breakfast fire just past the chuck wagon was still smoldering, and the cattleman hunkered down on his haunches, nodding toward a log for his guest to take.

Bark Rhine cleared his throat; he had a lot of phlegm, and turning his head slightly he aimed it at a clump of sage.

"You have easy traveling from the Panhandle?" he asked.

"Interestin', 'specially with some of the Kiowa and then the Comanche. Kept us moving. Lost a man down near the Arbuckle Pass."

"Lost?"

"Injuns, I dunno what tribe it was, Feller was one of my swing riders. Caught an arrow right in his Adam's apple. Poor sonofabitch."

Bark Rhine murmured something unintelligible.

"I'd figured on you being here a bit sooner," Rhine said. "But better late than never, as the saying goes."

"Well, the Injuns, like I told you. Then too, I didn't want to run weight off the beeves." He sniffed. "They look pretty good now. But after we got stampeded right after we crossed the Red, they was pretty damn gaunt. Lost nearly a half dozen head to the sonsofbitches."

They fell silent. Each feeling the other. It was in Bark Rhine's nature to talk, but he had learned the hard way as a young man that you got nowhere trying to rush an Indian or a cattleman. And he was grateful, for it was what had helped him survive his meeting with John Slocum. Who, he had told Cathy later, was about as talkative as a tombstone.

At length Bark Rhine commented on the good quality of the coffee and his host replied that it damn well better be good on account of cookie knew what would happen to him if it wasn't.

"You know, men working cattle and hosses don't want either perfume or piss when they're workin, but real Arbuckle. If you ken what I'm sayin'."

Bark Rhine nodded. "I do. I do know what you mean. And what is more, Parmelee, I appreciate your choice of the word 'ken'; a good, strong, old-fashioned word which I fear is rather swiftly falling into disuse. I am happy to see that men such as yourself are keeping it alive."

J. Parmelee didn't turn much of his attention to that remark, but instead took a drag from the cigarette that had been hanging on his lip.

"I ain't been up in this country since this good while,"

J. Parmelee said. "How's the town? How is it in Finality Gulch? Used to be a rip-roarer back in the old days when I was a saddle bum."

"There is a marshal. A good man. He—like a lot of lawmen—has trouble getting deputies, excepting of course when there's something like a necktie party. That seems to attract the upright, stolid, honest citizen."

He cleared his throat as he saw the cattleman looking at him as though he hadn't said anything. But Bark Rhine was a poker player through and through and so he waited.

About a minute passed and then J. Parmelee spoke. "What did you want to see me about? Fred Bass told me to hold the herd here at the creek and you'd meet me. I am here and the herd is here. Better tell me what's up."

Bark Rhine cleared his throat, then took a puff at his cigar. "Mr. Bass is a business connection of mine—in a way. We now and again work together. I happened by chance to hear that he had this herd of cattle coming up from Texas and—well, to make a long story short—we got together and worked out a plan." He paused, taking a drag on his cigar. He examined the ash, but did not tap it off, then resumed, indicating his remarks with gestures of the cigar.

"You'll be driving the beeves through Finality Gulch, right down the middle of Main Street to the railroad pens for shipping."

"That's what Bass told me." He ground out his cigarette between his callused thumb and forefinger and dropped it. Then reaching to his shirt pocket he brought forth a plug of chewing tobacco. "I don't see where you fit in, Mister Rhine."

"I don't, as you say, fit in anywhere. I am running the whole operation. Bass is working for me, and so—

if I might put it crudely—so are you, Parmelee."

He watched it hit the bony man.

"I had thought Bass would have made that clear to you."

"He did," J. Parmelee said. "I was just checking it."

"Makes sense," Rhine said in a cold voice. "I want you to bring the herd in from the north end of town. There will be men there—my men—to help you drive them down Main Street."

"That the only way to get to the yards?"

"It is the way I want it." Rhine took the cigar out of his mouth after he had said those words, and studied the lighted end. Then, as though speaking to the cigar he said, "I happen to know that three of your men have already been to town. And raised hell in one of the saloons."

"Couldn't be helped," J. Parmelee said. "The men are feisty as all hell. It's been a real long drive, and hard to boot."

"You know a man named Slocum?" Rhine suddenly asked.

"I have heard of him."

"What have you heard?"

"He is no man to mess with."

"That's right."

"He working with you, is he?"

Bark Rhine didn't answer this immediately. He took a slow drag on his cigar, and again studied the ash.

"Mr. Parmelee, John Slocum at this point is an unknown quantity in our—uh—operation. He . . . well, let me put it this way: at this moment let's assume he might be a problem. I want you to be prepared—and your men also, of course—to deal accordingly." His eyes lifted to regard the cattleman.

"Huh," said J. Parmelee. And then again, "Huh . . ."

"I expect that—if anyone should happen to cause

you any difficulty in the execution of your task, your work, your duty, that you would deal with him as necessary." He paused. "Is it clear? Do I make myself clear?"

"Just let me know when to start the herd."

"Probably in the next few days, but I will get word to you."

"Good enough."

"And it'll likely be around noon."

"Noon?"

"Towns are sleepy around noontime."

12

The noon stage made history in Finality Gulch on that particular day. Although as some more precise reports had it, it wasn't exactly the Butter & Eagle Stage that created history. Indeed, as some more serious citizen later pointed out, events don't make history; people do. It was a point not really necessary to prove to anyone. All that counted with the citizens of Finality Gulch was that the bewitching redhead with the ostrich plume in her hat and the small monkey in her arms did more for the life of Finality that afternoon than an army of victorious cavalry would have managed. The ripple of excitement that started as she got off the stage at the depot turned into a wave as she walked a block from the Finality Gulch stage office to the Great Hotel. Drunks and mischievous boys alike followed her and laughed and pointed rudely when the monkey bared its teeth at them and made strange jungle sounds they'd never heard before. Some of the mob even shoved its way into the lobby of the hotel, all but brushing against the ravishing young lady, and breathing on her as she bent over the hotel's register to sign her name.

The gang soon discovered that she was no one to try to push around. Turning on them, her cheeks reddening with sudden anger, her voice rose just enough to let them know what she was feeling. She was clearly too much of a lady to lose her temper.

"Is this the way you treat ladies in this town? Now get out of my sight! Go! Go away!"

Her action was so surprising that the crowd did indeed break up. Some left the premises, but others stayed around, riveted with curiosity. As she started back across the lobby after signing the register, leaving instructions with the porter about her baggage, some bold individual, fortified no doubt with whiskey courage, leaned over the register and read aloud the new arrival's name.

"Alice Rivers, London, England." Turning then to the small crowd that had lingered, he demanded to know who had ever heard of such a place. His sally nearly brought the group to the floor with mirth. And their raucous reaction carried back through the small crowd like a thinning wave, out into the street.

About an hour later, in the middle of the afternoon, the lady—without her chatty monkey—took the entire clientele of the Generosity Saloon completely by surprise as she walked through the swinging doors. She pushed through the crowd to take a position right smack behind a draw poker player who was evidently seriously considering laying down his hand in the face of a one thousand dollar raise.

The player involved in this predicament was Mr. Bark Rhine, who became immediately aware that someone was standing behind him, and he looked around. Of course, it was not proper for someone to stand directly behind a player in a game of poker. General looking was acceptable, but to crowd up as close as the lady from London, England had done was to break an unwritten law. And the crowd of onlookers waited to see what Bark Rhine would do.

To everyone's surprise, Mr. Rhine appeared quite pleased to find the beauty standing that close to him, and he smiled a greeting at her. Then, turning back to his table companions he said, "It's got to be my lucky day, boys. I'll call and raise it a thousand."

One of the players said, "Looks like you can beat kings over tens, Mr. Rhine. It's all yours."

Bark Rhine leaned forward and pulled in the pot. Then he laid his cards face up on the table. He had jacks over tens.

The player he'd backwatered shoved back his chair, stood and stalked angrily out of the saloon.

The crowd instantly became a rumble of excited noise about the game, Bark Rhine's bluff, and the ravishing redhead who to all appearances had brought on the dramatic moment.

A good while later the same day, the lady in question and the gentleman who had raked in those respectable winnings were seated in the gentleman's office at his ranch discussing matters important to both.

"It went well," Bark Rhine was saying. "And it was good the way you had them with their tongues hanging out. But of course, you've got to understand that no one—I mean, *no one*—must know any connection between the two of us."

She was seated in the chair that normally was placed in front of his desk, but which Slocum had moved alongside it. The gentleman in residence apparently had decided to leave it there.

"It was a good, though modest beginning," Rhine continued, his eyes warmly taking in her figure and her lovely face while at the same time fully aware that he was not dealing with any dumbbell. She had followed his instructions to the dot. He was pleased that his gamble had come out this well.

"And so what you're saying," she said, leaning a little forward in the leather chair, "is that this man Slocum is your target."

"He is *a* target. *The* target is something else."

His eye dwelt momentarily on the curve of her cheek where it met the corner of her eye. And suddenly he was thinking of Catherine and their most recent encounter. Well, he had better keep his thoughts on business. And the business at hand was especially important.

"I want you to try to meet Slocum," he finally said.

"Yes, I gathered that."

"You are intelligent," he said.

"Yes, I know. So what is it you want me to find out?"

"Anything and everything you can about him," he said, stifling his annoyance at her sureness. Well, she would have to learn. Damn some women; just because they were good looking they thought they could run things. Well, she'd have to sing a different song if she was going to continue working with him. Again. She had been damn good at what he'd given her thus far as well as in the past. He had no complaints.

"This matter," he said, employing a grave tone and serious face to impress the importance of the "game," as he called it to himself. "This matter is of the utmost importance."

"What do you want me to do? I mean aside from getting next to this man Slocum."

"Getting next to him?" His eyebrows lifted.

"Getting acquainted with him. Getting to know him. Why, were you thinking of more than that?"

And she didn't appear to be the least disturbed at the thought that he might.

"No, my dear. No. Nothing especially personal, uh—unless necessary, of course. I leave that to your discretion. I must say that this Slocum is clearly a man of appetite. Sexual appetite. And so it might be necessary to, uh. . . ." He let it hang, thus insinuating much more than could actually be spoken out loud and face-to-face.

"Can you tell me some more about him. In fact, can you give me a little more of a general picture of the operation? I am not nosy, as you must realize by now, but the more material I have at hand the clearer I can be in making decisions."

"I will make the decisions, my dear," he said, cutting in suddenly in a stronger tone of voice than he had yet used. And he watched the color come to her face. Good! The bitch needed a checkrein. Just like anybody else.

"You might work some of the poker games. Try the Generosity—you've had a taste of the place. And one or two of the other places. But be careful." He paused, stretching both arms out with the heels of both hands on his desk while he drummed his fingers. "As you know, the frontier is changing, and women are coming into . . . uh . . . more respectable levels. Such as gambling. Poker Alice is of course a fixture, Calamity Jane, Madame Moustache, and the others. I, of course, do not put you in that category, for you are far and away higher, above that level. But you will attract notice. As indeed you most certainly did today. They will in due course come to you."

"They? Who are 'they'?"

"The people we are interested in. The people I need to know more about."

"Like Slocum?"

"Like Slocum. Though he will be the one exception; that is, the one you will go out of your way to have him meet you. If you understand what I am saying."

"I would be deaf, dumb, and blind if I didn't," she said caustically. "So would my monkey, Rodolfo."

He controlled the surge of anger that rose in him and made a mental check on the debit side for her. She'd probably need taking down. Well, it would be his pleasure. The thing was, she'd done such good work those last two times.

But he did have the last word, saying, "I am not concerned as to whether or not your monkey can understand what I am trying to get across to you, but whether you do." And then, with flawless timing he added, "My dear . . ."

Reaching to his waistcoat he removed his watch and took his time studying it. All as part of the atmosphere he wished to establish for his meetings with her.

Raising his eyes as he slipped the watch back into his pocket, he watched her closely.

Yes, he could see that he had gotten under her skin more than a bit. Good enough. One had to handle the hired hands with a firm hand. Otherwise . . . well, otherwise, you found yourself with too many uncontrollable ends and you ended in the famous soup. As he continued to sit there watching her, he let time work for him. She began to shift her weight, and then she studied the back of her right hand.

"Is there anything more?" she asked him finally.

He simply shook his head slowly. "No," he said softly. "Only your report to me. That's the next step." Then he leaned forward onto his desk suddenly. "Oh, but remember that time is important. Things have to come together within the next very few days. I need material from you regarding Slocum and . . . uh . . . a man of whom you may not yet have heard."

"Who? Has he got a name?"

"Indeed he does. It is Ridey Bones. What I want is for you to see what people in town think of him. If indeed they are thinking anything. They may not have heard of him. But on the other hand, there are bound to be people who have. And who might be quite talkative. I want everything you can get. Not only the actual words spoken about him, but the attitudes—the in-between things as it were—about the man. I believe you know what I mean."

"I do."

"I want facts, and I also want opinion, rumor, even lies. It doesn't matter. I want to know how much people are talking about him. This of course goes for Slocum too. What the gossip is on him. What is sure."

He saw that she was a good listener, and so he leaned forward again, this time in a more confiding posture.

"You see, just the bare facts about a person can be useful but also very dull. People are like paintings of themselves. A good painting will remind you of what has been left out. The same when you describe a person. You learn from the shading, the emphasis on this point as opposed to that; this gossip and that. Everything is important if you want to understand people and their situations. Because the person is the situation and the situation is the person."

A silence fell, and he could see her taking it all in. Of course he had no idea whether she would accept or reject on some of the things and people he mentioned. But it was her reaction that was important to him.

He nodded then, and she stood up. By golly, he was thinking, she's a damn good looking piece of woman. Well, he had Catherine. Of course, if anything happened to their situation, well, there was this—standing right there in front of him. But he was a religious man and so he put all such thoughts swiftly out of his mind.

On the way to the door he said, "Oh, and there's just one more thing."

"I thought there might be," she said smiling.

"That's one for you then," he said, also smiling, but without warmth. "There is one other person I want you to keep a line on. And to keep in touch with me about him."

His hand was on the doorknob.

"Does this person have a name?"

He opened the door and she walked into the hallway outside his office.

"Oh yes, his name is Otis."

"Otis? That the first or last name?"

"It's the whole shootin' match," Bark Rhine said. "I want everything you can get on him."

"His personal life?"

"Like I said a moment ago, my dear. If necessary."

She was just a little shorter than he was, and now she stood facing him directly. Her hands were at her sides. and her head was bent just slightly to one side.

"Where will I find this gent? Any special hunting ground he favors?"

"The Generosity, like everybody else. But also the other saloons. And who knows where else. He is not someone I know intimately after all."

"Otis . . ." She pushed her tongue into her cheek so that it looked like she had a ball in her mouth. "Does the gent go by any other names?"

"I don't know. Otis could be his first name or his last. Or maybe he isn't Otis at all. The only real thing I can tell you is that he can shoot an eyelash off a prairie dog without making the animal blink."

13

Slocum had just ridden across the wooden bridge when he saw the rider high up on the other side of the river, cantering down the rough trail. At first he didn't recognize the rider, but he drew rein, still on the approach to the bridge from the side of the mountain that led up to Ridey Bones' place. He realized it was a woman riding, and that it had to be the girl. She was riding the little blue roan.

Swiftly, but not without care, he checked his back trail, and studied the trail ahead of him that led up a long draw into the wide stand of timber—spruce and pine mostly—and would then become pretty narrow. It was the best way to approach Ridey's outfit from Ridey's standpoint, the advantage being that anyone coming up the narrow, heavily overgrown trail would have a tough time making it in silence and with any degree of certainty that he was on the right path. Meanwhile, anyone at the Double C would have little trouble being able to spot the rider's progress by staying lined up with the series of giveaway spots where anyone on the trail could be seen from the ranch. Provided of course that the person at the outfit knew exactly where to train his glasses.

Only a minute later he felt something inside him tighten as he realized it had to be Janey. Instantly he checked the impulse to start up the trail to meet her, deciding instead to wait for her. He felt uneasy, but he couldn't quite put a name on it. He saw nothing suspicious when he checked what he could see of her back trail. And then he wondered if maybe something had happened to either Ridey or his wife. For it was clear that the rider was not out enjoying a ride. She was heading somewhere. He waited, every now and then checking her back trail, and noticed more of her as she got closer. He made sure that she didn't see him, just in case somebody was behind her.

In another twenty minutes or so, she rode out of the stand of trees and he called to her. The first thing he noticed was the shock in her face, in her whole body. And when she saw him he could see her agony.

"John! Is it really you? My God, I was coming to find you . . ." And she broke into tears while he brought his horse right alongside the blue roan and put his arm around her.

"What happened? Are you all right?" He leaned back a little to take a look at her.

"It's Grandpa, it's Mister Bones . . ." she blurted out. "Oh John. They beat him. He is hurt. I was going for you, and for a doctor—I thought at Pitchfork. I don't know. He made me promise not to ride over to the Rhine ranch. But he can hardly speak. And I'm worried about Gram too. And . . . oh, I wanted to talk with you so much! And you haven't been there, though I knew you would come. And I . . . I . . ." And she began sobbing uncontrollably.

He leaned back in his saddle now. "Was there anyone else around? I mean when you left the outfit?"

"Those men—there were three of them, but one in

particular. He was kind of the leader. He wanted to know where you were. And they rode off. I've got to get a doctor. I have got to get to town."

"That will take us a good while. I think the best thing is for me—both of us—to get up to the house and see how he is."

She started to protest, but he pointed out to her that it would be best if he could take a look at Ridey and then maybe if necessary bring him into town either on horseback or maybe in the wagon.

She saw the sense in that, and they started back up the trail to the ranch.

"Oh, I feel so relieved," Janey said, and gave him a shaky, though fond smile.

The sun was getting close to the rimrocks and the light was changing.

"We'll make it in good time," he said.

"I'll cook you up some good supper. I'm so glad to see you." And she was almost laughing, though obviously still worried about Ridey.

"You have any notion who the men were?" he asked.

She described them, but it didn't help.

"I don't know their men," he said. "But were there any of the ones who rode by the other night when I was first there? Do you remember?"

"I don't believe so. But I could be wrong. I was very excited that time and probably didn't notice what I should have noticed, had I been more calm. I was worried then about Millie."

"And they didn't say anything about coming back? Did they threaten you or speak to you at all?"

"Not to me. But they told Ridey that if he didn't do what they wanted that next time they'd beat him harder. Oh . . . oh, it was awful. I didn't see it actually happen. I was up getting firewood for the house and they just rode in fast, did what they did, and went away. And they told him to keep his mouth shut. I guess it was a warning."

"Did Ridey say anything about what they'd said to him?"

"He just cursed them mostly. But he could hardly speak. Oh my God, it was awful." And she started to sob again.

After a moment she had control of herself. And he asked her if she thought she would recognize any of the three men if she should see them again. She said she thought so.

As they reached the first gate leading into the Double C, he opened it without dismounting, and closed it the same way.

The day was waning now, and the evening star was clear and alone in the sky.

"I could use me some vittles," Slocum said, shrugging off the heavy mood that had been with them all the way up the side of the mountain.

"I'm so happy to see you I'll cook you up something really good. Well," she added. "I hope it'll be good. I hope . . . *you* will like it."

"I will like it," he promised, smiling across at her. "But right now, I want you to stop worrying, sit easy on your pony, and if you see anybody around the place who doesn't belong there, don't say anything. I will handle it."

He looked across at her and was pleased. His effort to relax her a little had worked, and now he saw that she was alert again and sharp, but without so much tightness in her face and her body.

Tip, the black, white, and brown cattle dog ran out to greet them, barking an alarm to the people in the house, and seeing who it was, wagging his tail.

Slocum knew they had to be watching the place, but there was no other way to go. He had to see how Ridey was, and Millie. It had crossed his mind to send the girl into town, but she wouldn't have arrived before dark and he wasn't sure how she'd be treated. Especially, if the boys ran into her.

He was prepared for the worst after he stripped both horses and walked up to the house. To his surprise he found his host in better shape than he'd imagined. The old boy was propped up in bed and was talking to his wife, scolding her for letting Janey take off for a doctor.

"Ah! There you be! I see you got a good doctor!" as they both walked into his bedroom. "I'm doin' fine an' I expect to be up and about come Thursday, Wednesday, whatever it is by tomorrer or day after. I'll get them sonsofbitches if it's the last thing I do on this here . . . !" He fell into an attack of coughing which all but paralyzed him with pain, followed by heavy breathing and deep swearing.

"Good to see you're feeling better," Slocum said. "I've come back to hang in there as your ramrod."

" 'Bout time, by God. Wondered where the hell you'd got to." And he glared fiercely at Slocum. "Told you I'd hired you on for whatever price you like and which I can afford. And, by jingo, first crack out of the box and you take off."

"I was trying to get a line on what's going on around here," Slocum said, without the least sign of apology in his manner. "And I do believe I told you I'd be workin' part-time and however I was able, on account of I have some work of my own I got to attend to." And he cocked his head and grinned at the impatient patient.

"What did you find out?"

But Slocum saw that he was getting weak, and he decided it would be better to wait till morning.

"I'll talk it over with you in the morning," he said, looking at the two women for support.

They were quick to fill the breech. Millie started fussing with his covers, to his great irritation. "I want another drink," he snorted. "The booze helps more than any damn new fangled medicine."

Shortly after that he was asleep. In fact, he fell asleep right in the middle of a sentence.

Millie picked up the bottle and glass on the table beside his bed and sighed.

"At his age. You know, he still thinks he can fight and do all the things he used to do."

Something in her tone caught Slocum.

"Like in the old days," he said. "They're like that, aren't they, some of those tough old boys?" And he smiled warmly at her, hoping she would open up.

But she only shook her head and walked out of the bedroom, carrying the bottle and glass like it was something to dispose of permanently.

Slocum turned a different smile on Janey, who returned it with a dazzling one of her own.

Then she said, "Maybe he'll sleep now. And we could have some supper. Gram invited you very definitely, now that you're one of the household."

He tried again at supper to draw the old lady out, with partial success. She did get as far as referring to how her husband "Used to ride with some of the wild ones."

"Did he ever mention a man named Otis?" Slocum asked at one point. "Or have you ever heard of him?"

She simply didn't answer the question, and so he did not pursue it. Then he asked her if she recognized any of the three men.

"No."

He wanted to ask if she had heard of Jake Whistler, but for some reason—he wasn't really sure why—he just had the feeling it wasn't the right time. Maybe it was because there was too much else going on. What she needed now was light talk. And he gave it, telling them both how it was up north around the Sweetwater country, and then relating some of his more acceptable adventures on various cattle drives and in some of the towns he'd seen.

It worked. By the end of the meal, they were both much more relaxed. Millie even gave him a small smile as she excused herself, saying she was going to "Lie down a spell," after checking on Ridey to see that he was comfortable.

"I'll do the dishes," Slocum said to Janey. "You've had a rough day, so why don't you just head for bed? I'm planning to stay up a while to keep an eye on things."

She seemed to hesitate. But then she nodded. "Good," she said. "Good. Make yourself at home then."

In the morning the old man was better. When Slocum walked into the room where he was lying on his back in bed, he found those eyes directly on him and they were full of life. No question at all but that the man was a tough one.

"What you up to, young feller?" The words were not all that strong, but the man behind them was, Slocum told himself.

"I am still wondering about this feller I asked you about."

"Who? You asked me more questions than I could shake my pecker at, for Chrissakes."

Slocum couldn't resist smiling at him. But old Ridey Bones maintained his stern, grainy demeanor.

"All you young fellers do nowadays is ask questions," he said. And he nodded his gray head. Then cut his eye fast to Slocum. "Exceptin' yerself isn't one nor t'other," he went on. "Fact, yer both at the same time. Where you from, mister?"

"From right here," Slocum shot back and grinned.

The old man lying in the bed chuckled at that, then started to laugh harder. Suddenly he became locked in pain and started cursing.

At this point his wife entered and bawled Slocum out. Ridey, recovering from his attack, roused himself sufficiently to defend his new foreman.

Finally, Slocum settled the whole event by leaving the room and returning shortly with coffee.

"I'll get some food on the table," Millie said.

Slocum grinned at the old man in the bed. "Peace is here again," he said. "I should be more careful."

"Ach!" the crusty, gnarled figure in the bed said. "You can't live with 'em, and you can't live without 'em!" And his ancient face creased into what Slocum took to be a sort of wry smile.

At that point Janey walked in and said good morning to both of them, holding Slocum's glance just a little longer to let him know how much she had enjoyed his visit to her bed during the night.

Slocum found himself beaming at her, and then caught himself, hoping the man in the bed hadn't noticed. But fortunately Ridey was busy cursing his aches and pains.

"Can I help?" Slocum asked.

"Just by staying with Grandpa," she said. "Thank you." And again her smile went right through him, bringing him back to the long tussle they'd had in her bed. The memory of her flesh, her breath, her touch, and the smell of her sex drove his trousers into a fantastic rigidity which he trusted the man in bed did not notice. But he knew the girl did as she blushed and hurried out of the room.

Over coffee with Ridey he calmed down. The women were out in the kitchen, and the old man was dozing, but now and again he awoke and looked at Slocum, who was seated in a chair close by.

"I'll take a look at the stock soon as I get this Arbuckle down," Slocum said.

"Good enough."

"You want anything?"

"I do."

Slocum cut his eye fast at his tone of voice.

"I want them sonsofbitches right at the end of my goose gun. I will get them. I promise you that, my lad."

"Wait. Wait till you're better."

"Oh, I will. Don't worry. They really got me mad this time. And I'll be patient. I won't spoil it by going up agin 'em before I be ready."

"You know them."

"Like they was sitting right where you are."

"They regulars with Rhine? You know them from before?"

"Before?"

"Before all this trouble about wanting your spread."

"No. They're new. Hired guns, like you said yerself when you spotted them. I'll get 'em. And I'll get that sonofabitch Rhine to boot."

"I can't figure why they want your outfit," Slocum said, seizing the opportunity to get into some of the things he wanted to say.

"What do most men want in this here country?" Ridey asked, looking Slocum right in the eye.

"Grass. Water."

"That's for sure," Ridey Bones had lain back and spoken those words to the ceiling.

"And what else?" he asked, still gazing up as he lay back on his pillow.

"Gold."

Silence.

"Are you telling me there's gold around these parts?" Slocum asked. "If there is some people who combed through here not too long ago sure missed it. Everybody knows there is no gold in this part of the country. Are you telling me now there is?"

A silence followed these words and Slocum didn't pursue it. But he was damn sure of what he had said, for the question had come up only about a year ago, as it did periodically in various places all over the West. Gold! The big hope.

"Everybody thinks there's just got to be another Black Hills," he said. "And wishful thinking has driven a helluva lot of men to hell."

"That's what I know, too," said Ridey and a sound now came from him that Slocum took to be a chuckle.

"You're saying there is gold."

Silence.

Then, "In a sort of way of speakin'."

"Holy Moses!"

"Moses got nothin' to do with it, mister."

Slocum leaned forward in his chair now. "Are you telling me that there is a gold strike around here—and maybe on your land!"

An expression now came into the old man's face that Slocum took to be a mixture of humor and surprise, but the old man said nothing.

"Listen. People have been over this country with all kinds of mining men and even holy men looking for gold. And nobody—I will say it again—*nobody* has ever found one fingernail of the yellow stuff. Come on, now!"

The man in bed was grinning at him.

"Look. The only way gold could be in this kind of rock that's up here is if . . ." And he stopped cold as it hit him.

A chuckle came from the battered figure in the bed. "Shit take it, it hurts like a bitch to laugh."

"Are you telling me somebody's salted a gold mine somewhere around here?"

Ridey Bones lay there sucking his teeth loudly, which Slocum had noticed he did quite often.

" 'Course, it ain't known. 'Course, there won't be many believin' what I have been tryin' to tell a smart young feller like yerself there . . ."

They fell silent then. Slocum was trying to remember something he had heard about a hidden treasure or a cache of gold—something—in the area of Finality Gulch, but it kept eluding him.

They were silent for a while, and then Janey entered, bringing them more coffee. That stirred the man in the bed to chuckle, even though it obviously was painful for him.

"You figgered it out, have you? You looking for Otis. You asking about Jake Whistler. I could tell you plenty."

And for the first time Slocum began to wonder how much liquor Ridey Bones had been taking in. Was he drunk? His words were a bit slurred, but only occasionally. He was obviously tired and in a good deal of pain. So the booze had helped. Yet the old man seemed now to have taken a bit more than was necessary.

Well, Slocum thought, maybe all to the good. But if the old man—old Ridey Bones, who'd ridden with Jake Whistler—knew something about hidden loot, did it mean the cache was on the Double C range? It sure looked like it. But something like the discovery of hidden treasure wasn't something you could keep secret. And he had never heard even a hint of such a thing.

And yet why was Bark Rhine on the scene? He knew as much about ranching and raising stock as Slocum knew about knitting. Just what was that bugger doing here in this country, trying to buy out Ridey Bones?

And not only did he try to buy the old man out, but when that wasn't possible, he used threats and finally harassment—like the riders that had come on his first night at the Double C—and now the beating.

What was Rhine up to? And why had he wanted Slocum to join him? What was his plan?

Slocum had asked around some in town but about all he could pick up was that Rhine was an operator who pulled deals on all levels—animal stock, banking, running a stage line, and lots more in a number of places in the West.

On top if it, what did Heavy Hank Finnegan want with him? He had said he wanted him to locate Otis. Well, he knew now that Otis was indeed in this part of the country: in fact, in Finality Gulch. But a lot of people could have found that out. And he was pretty damn sure that Finnegan had known that too. But for some reason he'd wanted Otis "located", he'd wanted to know his moves. Moves toward the "gold" that Ridey had indicated? Or, moves toward bringing Otis back to Laramie? Except that the fact was that Otis had served his time. He hadn't escaped, as had been reported. He had been legally released. And evidently had headed instantly for Finality Gulch. He had returned to the stamping ground of the old Whistler gang.

Slocum had discussed this with Ridey Bones, but he hadn't gotten very far. Until today. Evidently, the booze had helped.

Looking up now he found the patient's eyes on him. Ridey had had a snootful, no doubt about it. Drunk. Well, when a man got beaten up like that, especially an old man, then a little booze couldn't hurt. And if it was the thing that did help, then more power to drink and drinker. Pain, Slocum was well aware,

loosened more tongues, one way or another, than anything else.

"Tell me about the gold, Ridey," Slocum said,
figuring he had nothing to lose by a direct approach.

"Hah!" The old man's cackle broke like a bunch of
falling stones into the room. "I knew it. You're after it
too, hah!"

"No." Slocum shook his head. "I'm trying to locate
Otis, then I can move on to the Sweetwater, which
was where I was heading in the first place. Now I've
been sidetracked with fist fighting, a cattle stampede,
a shooting, you getting yourself beaten up, and who
knows what else that's been going on behind my back.
I am just looking for a little hint of what the hell
is going on here. I don't want anything for myself. I
am looking forward to being shut of this town and
the assignment I was given, and getting on up to the
place I've been trying to get to since—since this good
while."

His speech carried passion and Ridey was clearly
impressed. His mouth fell open, his eyes popped a
little.

And suddenly they both burst out laughing.

"Mister . . ." And the old man was wiping tears from
his eyes. "Mister, you have made your point."

"The Lord be praised."

"Amen . . ."

And they both burst into laughter again.

Now they were silent as darkness entered the room
with the sun having moved further west. Presently
Millie Bones came in with a coal oil lamp and set
it down on the table next to Ridey's bed and lighted
it.

"He won't let me send for the doctor," she said.

"By the time he'd get here he'll be all on the mend,"
Slocum said. "I think he's doing fine. Just needs some

rest from those cuts and bruises. Or did you find something broke?" he asked suddenly.

"I don't believe anything is broken," she said. "Thank the Lord. What he really needs is rest. And . . ." She reached over and picked up the nearly empty bottle of whiskey. "And less of this!"

Swift as light that old man's hand whipped out and grabbed the bottle, pulling it under his bedclothes.

"Quicker on the draw than Wild Bill, by golly," said Slocum in admiration.

And all of them broke into laughter, though Millie was trying not to.

Slocum, who had his back to the door, was happy to hear Janey in that medley of mirth and now offered her a chair.

"Thank you, but I have some things I have to attend to." And she was gone again, leaving for him a part of her delightful atmosphere which included not only her good looks, but her sound and scent. And whatever it was about her that he found unnameable and compelling.

When his thoughts left her after a moment he was aware that Ridey Bones was watching him.

"Reckon you must of figgered by now she ain't my granddaughter, nor Millie's, as a matter of fact."

Slocum nodded.

After a short silence Ridey spoke, with his eyes on the ceiling as he lay back on his pillows. "She come out here not so long ago looking for her pa."

"And you're covering her with the granddaughter business."

Ridey Bones sniffed.

"She was looking for an old associate of mine, though she don't know that, exceptin' I reckon by now she suspicions it."

"Jake Whistler."

The old man looked directly at him now. "Mister, you are no dumbbell. I might of knowed it couldn't be hid."

"Those things ain't easy to hide," Slocum said. "They sort of have an atmosphere or something about them, and people cotton to what's going on before you know it."

Ridey reached under the covers and drew out the bottle. His eyes were watching the door as he offered a snort to his companion.

"Sure. I'll join you," Slocum said. And he accepted the bottle, as Ridey inclined his head toward the door as a sign of caution.

The swig was warming, and Slocum was glad for it. He handed back the bottle and watched the man in bed take a hefty drink, then fall into a fit of coughing, causing the room to reek of alcohol.

"Got hair on it, by God," he gasped as the bottle disappeared beneath the covers again.

He was lying placid on his pillow, with eyes half closed as his wife Millie put her head in the door.

"Do you want anything, Ride?"

Ridey was silent, his eyes firmly closed. Then suddenly he started. "Eh? What's that? Ah? No, I don't need anything. Thank you, my dear."

His wife caught Slocum's eye, shook her head slightly from side to side and lifted her eyes toward the heavens as though searching for help, for a better understanding.

Slocum had a tough time controlling his laughter.

The instant she was gone, the eyes of the man in bed whipped open and he reached under the covers for the bottle.

"Better take it slow," Slocum said, and before the patient could object he went on. "You've got to keep sharp if we're going to trap the likes of Bark Rhine."

At those words the patient attempted to rise up, but had to give up and lie back.

"Take it slow," Slocum cautioned him again. "I am going to need you."

"Slocum . . . just who in the hell are you? You a lawman or somethin'?"

"Nope. I am just Slocum. Riding through. And I happened to run into you."

"But you were looking for Otis. I half figgered you were doing a little bounty hunting."

"That is not my line of work," Slocum said, and his tone of voice was not kindly, nor, for that matter, was the look he gave the old man.

"Phew!" said Ridey Bones. "You are a caution. I mean, you got more sides and corners and places a man don't see before he steps in 'em than a bear's got hair." He sniffed, reaching now to the pocket of his shirt very slowly.

"What are you looking for? A smoke?"

"My chewing equipment is what I'm after. You got my thinking all rubbed up. I got to take a look at things here for a minute." And he grinned at Slocum, muttering something Slocum couldn't quite catch.

"What say? Couldn't catch that!" And he leaned forward, his eyes directly on the man in the bed.

"I said you look to be a man who can tell the difference between a fly and an elephant, by God."

"I hope so," Slocum said carefully, checking the old man for hokum.

"I reckon you have got a pretty good picture of the lay of the land hereabouts. I been wonderin' . . ."

"Wondering whether you might throw in with me, and maybe me with yourself. That it?"

"You hit the nail. Shit, 'less we're open with each other we could be going in different directions."

"At cross-purposes," Slocum said.

"How's that?"

Slocum didn't answer. Instead he said, "Tell me about the gold."

"I can tell you about the gold rumor," the old man said carefully.

"Shoot."

"There has been a rumor for some good long while now that Whistler and his gang left a lot of loot somewheres, maybe where they used to have their roost."

"Where was that?"

"Rabbit Trap. Not far from here; matter of fact it's s'posed to be on my land, though it's something to argue on. Thing is, it's close enough that I'm in the picture. You got me?"

"I do. You're sayin' that whether anybody likes it or not, or whether or not the gold is actually on your range or just off it—and sometimes that's not so damn easy to figure—you have to be reckoned in on it."

"Right. Exceptin' I'm as welcome as an arrow straight up yer ass."

"I see. So now the question is not what they're going to do, but what are you doing about this event,"

All at once Ridey Bones sat up in bed looking at Slocum as though he'd been struck with the answer to the whole world.

"By God, you can say that again!"

Slocum chuckled. "Okay mister, but let's stop the funnin'. You and me got to start being serious with one another or we're in trouble. That feller Rhine is no dumbbell."

"And he sure ain't no angel neither," said Ridey Bones.

"So that's the rumor," Slocum said, "about the gold. Now then, what are the facts?"

But he didn't wait for Ridey to answer that, saying right away, "The fact is that whether there is gold or isn't gold doesn't matter any longer. What is important, what the real fact is, is that people *believe* there is gold. You got me?"

"Gotcha!"

"Now then, the question is does Rhine know for a fact about the gold or is he just building the rumor for his own purpose, the old shell game?"

"Uh-huh . . ."

"Do *you* know for a fact—yes or no—that there is gold there, or that there isn't?"

"I dunno." He cleared his throat, reached for the bottle, but left it as a thought occurred to him. "See, Jake used to use Rabbit Trap as his hole-in-the-wall. Fact, it really is a hole in the wall—from what I have heard, anyways. Lots of box canyons and a helluva job finding your way in or out if you ain't familiar with it. And the place is, or was, a fortress. Fact, it was a little town. Had a saloon, dancehall, houses, even a kind of general store. And nobody, least of all the law, had any suspicion of it. Until that rat sonofabitch Otis started puttin' on airs and one night, when he got up his courage with the booze, he braced Whistler."

The old man stopped, lips pursed in silence, his eyes squinting as he remembered.

"And . . ." Slocum prompted.

"And," said Ridey softly, speaking more like he was reliving the past. At least that was how it seemed to Slocum. "And he made the mistake of calling Jake Whistler."

The old-timer passed the bottle to Slocum, who accepted a swig, before refreshing himself. Then he continued.

"The stupid sonofabitch went to draw, but found himself looking into the dead man's hole—I mean looking right into the barrel of Jake's Colt .44. Jesus,

I never seen a draw that fast in my whole entire life, let me tell you."

"So what happened?"

"Jake told him to drop it on the floor. Which he did. Then Jake holstered his own weapon and told him to get out." He paused, squinting still, as if seeing the actual scene again. "But Otis suddenly reached for a hide-out and before you could say your own name, Jake had slammed him right in the throat. Then, by God he beat the living shit out of that mangy sonofabitch. It didn't take long, but Jake made him look like he'd been butchered." He stopped. "That was it. Exceptin' when he came to, and a lot of people had figured maybe he wouldn't. The whole saloon was taking bets on it. When he finally came to he swore he'd get even— or I should say when he got away from Rabbit Trap he made that threat or promise to somebody. That he'd by God even it. And he did. He shot Jake Whistler in the back. That came at a time when Jake told me he'd about had enough of the bandit's life and was thinkin' of headin' back East. I figgered he meant to his wife and kid. Though he didn't say that, I figgered it." He paused, and Slocum watched his old face working with that scene from long ago. "He never made it. That sonofabitch Otis shot him. Then it turned out he'd told the law about Rabbit Trap and we had one helluva time gettin' out of there." He looked suddenly hard at Slocum.

"I read what you're thinking," Slocum said. And he shook his head slowly from side to side. "I never heard a word of what you just said."

Ridey Bones nodded. For a while there was silence.

"There's no gold there," Ridey said finally. "There is something better than gold."

Slocum turned that over for a minute while the old man studied him.

"There's a stamp mill," Slocum said admiringly as it dawned on him.

"I knowed you'd figger it." Ridey grunted, then grinned and said, "took you a while didn't it."

"Hell, a stamp mill's the only way to handle stolen bars. Melt them down, eliminate the brand names, and you pretend you've found a mine. Neat."

"It was a secret for a long time," Ridey said. "Otis knew it, but I doubt anybody else that was about did. And for sure no one does now. You keep your eye out for Otis, Slocum. He's the type that gets jealous. He'll want to try you, he'll go up against you as sure as that horse of yours makes hoss apples." He coughed. "Mind me now, mister. Mind what I say to you. That Otis is no man to mess with. Best to stay away from him."

The two men continued to sit there; Slocum on the straight-backed chair that was covered in cowhide, and Ridey Bones sitting up in bed, leaning back against his pillows and a rolled blanket that Janey had brought and settled behind him.

As she did this none of the three spoke. And after the girl left the room the two men continued in their silence while the afternoon began to leave the window and the light changed to something softer. It seemed to Slocum it was the kind of light where a man felt himself more, more quiet, more—something else.

It was real good setting there, not saying anything, not really thinking about anything either; just being there as the room began to darken a little and without the slightest disturbance to either of the two men.

It was some while after Janey had left the room that Ridey suddenly spoke and Slocum knew he wasn't breaking the silence, but actually adding to it when he said, "I can sure see why Jake wanted to get back to her."

"So can I," Slocum said.

14

"I trust you have news for me, my dear." Bark Rhine smiled and settled himself down into his armchair and gave his full attention to the attractive redhead who was seated alongside his desk.

"It's been a while since we last talked, but I've had you on my mind," he continued as he studied her covertly.

"I've followed your suggestions." Alice Rivers, fondling the monkey that sat on her shoulder, smiled at the stocky little figure who had all the looks of a man of power and wealth. Which was what interested her. She had realized at an early age that she had a great need for money, and not very long after that interesting view into her own character came the revelation that she required, needed, the adulation of her fellows—especially men.

Rhine was smiling, admiring her looks, her figure, even her assured manner. He decided that he would have a little sport chopping her down, but not yet. He wanted her to give him her best while the situation was still forming. Still, things appeared to be coming quickly to a climax: all the pieces were falling into place, and then . . . well, maybe this piece who went by the name of Alice Rivers might be a little freshener from Catherine, who had been just a bit demanding lately.

"You have a line on Mr. Slocum, do you?"

"I do."

He leaned forward and picked up a pencil and began drawing on a pad that was lying in front of him. "What can you tell me? Did you . . . uh . . . have dinner, a cup of coffee; something of . . . uh . . . that nature?" And he allowed a little breathlessness in his voice so she would understand more deeply what he was after.

"Nothing intimate," she said. "I am not in that business, as I have told you from time to time."

He held up his hand instantly, all apologies. "But of course not! My dear, I had no intention of even suggesting such a thing. I meant, just a friendly, coffee or tea or whatever, something to grease the wheels of conversation."

He was shaking his head as though warding off such a terrible suggestion, which of course was the farthest thing from his mind.

"How did he strike you, my dear?"

"I haven't met the gentleman," she said calmly.

"But—but I thought you . . ."

"You asked me to get information that might be useful for you. Now, directly approaching a man like John Slocum—and I studied him for a while, here and there—isn't going to get someone like myself anywhere. What I did instead was to talk to a few people who were aware of him. And one way or another I learned a few things, and in particular one thing that might be of use." She paused, and her smile was brilliant; indeed, so brilliant he thought it might crack. And he felt his irritation rising. The snotty bitch! But he remained quiet.

"What did you discover, my dear?"

"He is staying at the ranch of a man named Ridey Bones."

"I already know that, my dear."

"He has been asking questions around town about a man named Otis."

"Yes, I know he has."

"The reason he happens to be in Finality Gulch is as a result of some arrangement he has made with a United States marshal in Ten Town by name of . . ."

"Finnegan," interrupted Bark Rhine, and there was victory in his voice. By God, she wasn't so damned smart as she thought she was. But it related to his rule. Always check, always test the person. Make sure, absolutely sure of the person's loyalty, not to forget intelligence.

"My dear, you've uncovered a great deal in a very short space of time, and I must admit that I am pleased with you. But yet, I have known all these things for quite some time."

He said it in an even tone of voice, with no criticism implied. He knew this was the best way to get the hook into the other person. No anger, no sarcasm, no reproach, just simple facts. The "Oh but of course, I knew that already" approach. It worked wonders in chopping a person down to size. Especially someone with just a little too much balls, like the woman in front of him. And yet, she was so goddamn good looking. He leaned back in his chair, absolutely brimming with satisfaction over his careful performance. Not an ounce of criticism, just the bare facts.

She was smiling, which he suddenly found difficult to understand. Anyone else in her position would be squirming. He looked at the monkey, now crawling up onto her shoulder and grabbing the back of her chair. Jesus, what a layout!

She was still smiling, with that arrogant tilt of her

eyebrows, while she fondled the monkey with one hand as she said, "I wonder if you happen to know that he has an interesting lady friend. I happen to have seen them together at the Best Food Cafe, having coffee together."

"And pray tell me how you see something compromising in that simple situation. There is certainly nothing singular in someone—a man—having coffee with a member of the opposite sex in a public cafe or restaurant. What do you see as, shall we say, incriminating?"

She was smiling. "Very simple. The fact that everything between them was so carefully *not* incriminating. You see, these are things that a woman would notice. But a man—never. It's much too subtle." And her smile was covering him like a sheet. He was furious as he felt her triumph.

However, at the same time, Bark Rhine was a man who more often than not knew better than to blow everything away through some reaction to someone trying to top him.

"Good work," he said. And in fact, a part of him meant it, even though it hurt to have her score like that. All the same, he was in business, and he knew now she was all she was cracked up to be. Definitely, he could use her.

"Who was the woman?"

"The granddaughter of the man, Ridey Bones. Or, his niece. I would have to check around to find out."

"Ah yes," he said, swiftly regaining ground. "Janey Sturgis, that's her name. She's out here from back east."

"She made some inquiries, some while ago around town about a man named Sturgis, possibly some relative. Does that name sound familiar to you?"

He shook his head.

"Slocum, by the way, has been scouting that herd of cattle that's been waiting outside town. I don't know if that information is of any use to you."

He nodded, now leaning forward onto his desk. "It could mean something. That happens to be a herd I've ordered for shipping. You see I'm planning to turn Finality Gulch into a shipping point for the Texas herds. This will be our first."

"I see. Now how do you wish me to continue? Stay on Slocum? Or see what I can find out about all these rumors that there just might be gold around here someplace or other?"

He stared at her then, trying to read her, but her face was as blank as an angel's.

"You'd make a good poker player," he said.

"I am a good player," she said.

"We'll have to have a game some time then."

"Any time you say, sir." And she started to sit up as though getting ready to leave.

The bitch, he was thinking, she wants everything on her terms, in her time, so that she decides.

She was standing now. He rose, came around the desk, and stood in front of her.

"I think that you've made a good start, my dear. Even though most of your material I was already aware of. Still, you fleshed out some of the interesting details."

He walked her to the door and now stood there with his hand on the knob. Suddenly, it seemed without either of them making a move, he had his arms around her and his erection pressing between her legs.

She reached down and unbuttoned his fly. In another moment, which, in its way seemed to him to be endless, though, not endless enough, she had his erection out of his pants and was down on her knees sucking.

It was all he could do to remain standing as he came, and came some more, and came again and again . . .

and again, while her monkey watched and scratched himself.

Some time later as he let her out, he bent to kiss her on the mouth, but she moved her head.

"Sorry, sir, I don't know you well enough to let you kiss me on the lips."

For a second or two he was stunned. "But—how about down there?"

"Any time, sir." And holding her monkey in her arms she smiled and stepped through the door. "I will see you when I get more information," she said. And Bark Rhine stood there in the doorway of his office feeling somehow that something had happened to him, but he wasn't quite sure what.

After she left, he stood there trying to calm himself. He tried to remember what he had to do this day— no, this morning. Returning to his desk he sat down, and made himself think about his plan. It helped drive her out of his mind. And in only a very little while he was his old self again. In charge. Everything was ready. The town council was under his thumb and J. Parmelee was just waiting for his word to move his herd down to the stockyards that had just been finished for such a purpose.

He was going over it to check for anything he might have omitted when there came a knock at the door. Swiftly he glanced at his watch.

"Come."

The square-shouldered, leather-faced man walked in. He had two guns tied down on his legs and wore an extra cartridge belt.

"You 'bout ready?" he asked as he sat in the visitor's chair without it being offered.

"Everything is ready. The question is are you ready?"

"I am. And it'll be noon tomorrow. That right?"

"You'll hear the cattle coming. They'll be moving through the town, down Main Street to the loading pens. At some point they will start to run and they will stampede right through the town. Now Parmelee and his men don't know this. You know it, you and your men. You will conduct the stampede. You will wait for my signal, which will be a pistol shot. And then you will fire and ride right through the town. Taking everything with you!"

"That is going to make one helluva mess," his visitor said, reaching up to pick his nose. He leaned his elbow on the arm of his chair while he examined what he had picked, then he flicked it away.

Bark Rhine managed to resist the temptation to rise and sweep off the top of his desk. But barely. Swiftly, he returned to the next day's action.

"I want those beeves to wreck the town. You understand. It should be an out-of-control thing. Then, just at the right moment, I'll have my deputies come in. They're ready."

"Deputies?"

He caught the alarm in his visitor's voice.

"They won't be real deputies. But appointed by myself who will take over as acting mayor. Since I am head of the council, with the mayor absent I have the authority to act as mayor."

"Where will the mayor be?"

"He will not be here," Rhine said and his words were hard.

"Hunh." He sniffed. "Hunh."

"You understand me, Otis. You understand how it will go?"

"Yeah. And I also understand Slocum will be there."

"He will be drawn away from the Bones' ranch when news reaches him that you will be in town and that there is a likelihood of trouble."

"And Bones?"

"Bones is injured. My men worked him over too hard, as I told you. You can catch Bones out at his place. I don't think he'll be in town."

"That sonofabitch!"

"That's it then." And Bark Rhine stood up.

But his guest remained sitting.

"I think we've covered everything," Bark Rhine said.

"The money. I want my money."

"We had agreed that you would be paid when the job was done."

The visitor was standing. "I want my money now, mister."

Bark Rhine hesitated. He was cursing himself for not having had some men in the room with him.

"Very well, I'll have to get it from my safe. Stay here and I'll only be a few minutes. Have a seat. I'll be right back." He started toward the door. "I'll be right back. And Otis, you understand there will be martial law declared in town following the stampede; and your uh—business with Slocum and Bones . . ." He paused, watching the other man's face working. "By the way, not that it matters particularly, but I didn't realize you knew Slocum."

"I don't."

"Yet you want to . . ."

"A favor for a friend." And his face parted in what Bark Rhine figured had to be a smile. "Besides, I get sick and tired of people telling me what a crack shot Slocum is. When I get done with him he'll be sufferin' from a bad case of lead poisonin'." And his voice rose in a giant cackle of laughter.

Suddenly he stopped. "Better get my money. I'll go with you." He grinned. "Just to keep you safe."

"I just remembered, your envelope is in the drawer in my desk," Rhine said.

"Better get it then."

Rhine walked quickly to the desk, keeping his hands carefully in sight, as with his right he reached to the drawer that was just in front of where he would be sitting if he were in his chair.

"That the drawer?"

"It is."

"Good enough."

Rhine reached into the drawer and brought out a large, thick envelope. "I'll count it," he said.

"I'll take it as it is," Otis said. "If it's not enough I'll let you know."

"It's the exact amount we agreed on."

"Fine. That's just fine." And he started to laugh. His laughter, Bark Rhine thought, sounded like a horse whinnying.

The transaction was over in a few minutes.

"See you tomorrow morning," Otis said at the door.

"The herd will come in at dawn."

"You already told me that."

"I expect you to do your duty well," Rhine said.

"I don't understand all that fancy talk, mister. Speak English to me."

"I'll see you in the morning at the north end of Main Street. My men will be placed all through the town. Everything is set to go very well."

"And Slocum?"

"He will be there."

"You sure? I wouldn't want to be disappointed."

"He will be told what's happening. He will know that you will be there and will challenge him. There won't be any mistakes."

"And Bones."

"I cannot be sure of Bones. The men really beat him badly. But you must find him afterwards if he doesn't show. Just remember that our agreement is that you get Bones, first and foremost."

"No—Slocum is the main target."

"Any way you like it, mister. Just so long as you earn your money. Fact, there will be a bonus for you."

"A—what?"

"Extra money."

The grin appeared again. "Good enough. Good enough."

And then Bark Rhine couldn't resist it. Almost before he even thought the words he was saying them. "Just like to say, watch out for Slocum. He is bad news. Draws faster than light. Takes two men to watch his draw: one when he goes for it, the other to see the other feller drop."

"I know somebody faster," Otis said, his face reddening. "You can stick around and watch."

That night they took a long time with it. They had the whole of the night together; all the time they needed. At first they caressed and she was instantly hot. So was he. And in a moment he had mounted her high and hard and all the way up to where he could rub the head of his cock on the innermost wall of her vagina.

She was moaning, trying to keep her voice down. He had to remind her that they might be heard, but then he almost gave them away himself. This time she caught him in time, covering his mouth with hers.

It was the best one.

"Each time is better than the last," she said. "Oh my God, you're so big!"

"You're so tight!"

"Too tight?"

"Oh God, no! Absolutely just right."

They stroked each other and tried different positions, different speeds. Actually, they worked in complete unison as their passion dictated the length of each movement of his huge erection and the delight they both knew as he drew it in and out with agonizing slowness. Finally neither could stand it any longer and they began to pump faster and faster and faster until it became more than either could endure as they fucked and fucked and fucked until, until. . . .

Until it became what it was supposed to become— impossible to endure even one split second more, and together they exploded, drowning each other with every drop of come that had built in them through their marvelous dance of love.

15

The mayor's office was empty save for Bark Rhine, his ranch foreman Hendry Jasper, and Clay Byles the town marshal. Tod Cameron, the mayor, had not been able to attend, due to sudden illness. It was not a serious illness, but it had been "suggested" by Mr. Rhine. The point being that meetings, as Rhine well knew, always went better when there was a minimum of alternate points of view. Tod Cameron invariably offered a certain opposition which was usually quelled by the presence of Bark Rhine. Occasionally Cameron influenced his fellow officials with the consequence that matters that should have easily slipped through became complicated, drawn out, and more often than not left a bad taste in the mouth of Mr. Bark Rhine.

Mr. Rhine lighted his first cigar of the day and was enjoying it.

"Gentlemen, we have very little to discuss. The situation is well in hand." He reached into his vest and took out a large silver watch—of which he was proud—and glanced at it. Lifting his eyebrows, he said, "Presently, gentlemen. Presently, I'd say within about twenty minutes to a half hour our plan will proceed as expected.

159

If Mr. Parmelee follows my instructions, which, of course, he will." He gave a little round chuckle to ease his words past any negativity that might have been festering at the way he had taken over the office of the mayor, placing the law entirely in the hands of Clay Byles. Even Hendry Jasper, the wholly reliable ramrod of the Rhine ranch, could see that was all that was necessary.

"You're seeing a new setup in Finality Gulch then," Clay Byles said. "Too bad Tod ain't here to celebrate it."

"He said he would try to make it, but he didn't sound too good when I talked to him last night." Bark Rhine beamed on his two companions, and looked around the room.

"We might have to elect or appoint a new council during the interim. And I think Clay here might take on one or two deputies. There could be trouble if there are malcontents in the crowd. But as I see it, and as I have told the Council for some time now, Finality needs law and order. It needs a strong hand at the helm because, gentlemen, we are growing. When we grow just a little more, you know, we can be in line for the county seat."

There came a knock at the door. When Rhine called out, it opened and a thin, bald man hurried in.

"The herd's on its way, Mister Rhine. You told me to tell you when."

"Good then." Rhine glanced again at his watch. "Where are they?"

"Joe Mitch, he just rode in saying they was at Shine Crossing. About twenty minutes away."

"Good enough. I am glad that Parmelee understood my suggestion to bring them in at noon. It's near noon now."

He stood up. "Byles, you had better check your men,

your deputies, and Jasper, you see to your bunch. Make sure that everyone is covered and that you know where they are. We can't take any chances with those wild Texans shooting up the town the way they did at Abilene and Honeytown."

"And Bixell," cut in Jasper. "The buggers treed the town, and kept 'er that way for nigh a week. That's what I heard tell."

"We will have nothing like that," said Bark Rhine. "We are here to protect our citizens."

He felt Clay Byles's eyes on him and turned to look at him. The marshal turned away.

As they walked down the bare wooden stairs they could hear, above the sound their boots were making, the distant rumble approaching.

They had almost reached the front door of the building when all at once it burst open and a man with a knit hat walked in. Seeing the party of three he came to an abrupt stop.

"What is it, Billings?" Rhine said.

"Mr. Rhine, they ain't bringing that herd around by the creek to get to the stockyard. They're figurin' on coming right down the middle of town."

"I am already aware of that fact, Billings." His tone was icy.

"But it's gonna raise hell with the town! All them cattle. What if they stampede?"

"Then there will be one helluva mess."

"But. . . ."

But the committee of three had already pushed past him, and were now out in the street.

"Check your men," Rhine said quickly to his two companions. "They should already be in their positions. I mean right now!"

Clay Byles, the marshal of Finality Gulch, and Hendry Jasper, the Rhine outfit's ramrod, were already on their way. Each was well attuned to the mercurial moods of their colleague, and had no wish to run afoul of him.

Now Rhine stood alone on the boardwalk outside the mayor's office. He could hear the rumble of the cattle—the hooves and bellowing making a distant drumbeat—and it was getting louder by the minute.

Now the street seemed to be filled with people. But he could hear Byles and some of his deputies warning everyone to get inside. The astonishment at having the cattle drive come right down Main Street seemed to paralyze a number of people, who continued to stand staring at where they expected the herd to appear at the western end of the town.

Suddenly he heard galloping from the other end of the street and turning, he saw four men riding hell-for-leather up the street toward the oncoming herd.

He recognized only the young hand who ran the livery stable when the regular man, Hank Wills, was drunk or just overslept, and the two other riders he didn't know. But the one in the lead, to his surprise, was John Slocum.

Rhine turned, looking for Hendry Jasper, but Jasper was long gone, checking on the men he had stationed along the route to make sure there would be no interference with the drive, no one being foolhardy enough to attempt to stop it.

But now Slocum and his companions had reached the leaders and were smashing at them with the knotted ends of their lariat ropes, trying to turn them before they could get to the main part of town.

At the same time, Jasper's men and some of Byles's deputies were firing at the herd with the purpose of stampeding them even more.

But Rhine could see that Slocum and his two helpers didn't stand a chance. They were being pushed back, even as they struck again and again at the charging leaders of the panicked herd.

And now suddenly, to his utter astonishment, he saw a wagon entering the street just about a hundred yards ahead of the first stampeding beeves. Nor could he believe his eyes as he saw it was being driven by the old buzzard Ridey Bones, and with some kid beside him.

Bones was lashing his team right across the street, and the moment they reached Clerk's Alley which ran alongside Gildersleeve's Store, he drew rein, climbed down—although slowly—to help the boy who was unloading some boxes.

The next thing he knew was that Slocum and his two companions had swerved to meet the wagon, jumped down from their horses and were pulling something out of the boxes.

Jasper came pounding up on his big bay horse. "They got dynamite, for Christsake!"

"Where the hell is Otis?"

But his voice was drowned as the first stick of dynamite hit just in front of the herd and exploded. Then another, and another; and the herd was plunging, rearing, the leaders getting trampled by the crazed beeves to their rear.

"Shoot those sonsofbitches with the dynamite, for Christsake!" screamed Rhine.

But the surprise had been too much for the men hired by Jasper and Byles. They had already emptied their guns.

But this didn't stop Rhine from screaming at them to "Get those dynamite bastards!"

But the herd had been stopped, and refused to move forward, even though some die-hard gunmen tried to get the stampede started again.

"You bastard, Slocum! You fucking bastard!" Rhine

screamed. "What the hell you think you're doing!"

"Stopping the stampede that you started, and saving the town from being wrecked, that's what I'm doing."

And John Slocum stood there in the middle of the street with a stick of dynamite in his hand, not yet lighted. But enough of Rhine's men had seen how fast he lighted the ones he had thrown, to keep their places.

It was then that the horrified eyes of Bark Rhine fell on the young boy who had been helping him. To his amazement, he realized it was a girl.

"Where the hell is Hendry? Jasper!"

And suddenly the street was silent.

"Where is Otis, God dammit! Where the hell is Otis?" Rhine was almost beside himself with rage and frustration.

His words—coming from the top of his lungs—fell into the street and died into silence.

"Otis is right here," a voice suddenly said, as the man himself stepped out into the street.

"Slocum!" His hard voice rang like a bullet down the stony street, waiting, and some people who spoke of it afterwards thought they heard its echo.

"I am right here," John Slocum said as he turned and faced the big man with the two tied-down six guns.

"I been waiting for you, Slocum. You sonofabitch."

They faced each other now in a silence that nobody could ever have measured.

Until at last it was broken.

"I been waitin' for you, too, you *dead* sonofabitch!" And John Slocum drew and nobody could later remember what they really saw. There was only the crack of the bullet from the .44 Colt, and the big man— known as Otis—fell dead to the street. His heavy body stirred a good bit of dust, later storytellers remembered.

• • •

In the evening he kissed her as they walked past the horse corral at the Double C.

"That was nice," she said softly. "You know, you're a very gentle man, John Slocum."

"If I am it's on account of you," he said.

"No," she said. "You're a very gentle man, Mr. Slocum."

"All right," he said. "But you are a very lovely young lady, Miss Whistler."

"It sounds funny to me, my real name," she said.

"You'll get used to it. It's a good name. From what I hear of Jake Whistler he was a good man."

They were silent and holding hands as they strolled.

"Ridey said you were—leaving," she said.

"I'll be heading north."

"Whereabouts?"

"The Sweetwater."

"What's that?"

They had stopped just inside a line of trees where they were hidden from anyone who might pass by.

"It's—well, it's the Sweetwater, that's what it is." And he kissed her again.

He was already undressing her, slowly, but without hesitation.

Then he said, "I ain't askin' you to throw in with me, excepting maybe I thought you might like to take a look at the Sweetwater country. I mean maybe for a spell."

"You like the Sweetwater, don't you?"

"Some old-timer I once met said, 'There ain't any-place like the Sweetwater anywheres.'"

"Well, maybe I might take a look at it—just for a spell."

"Good enough then," he said. And he put his arms around her. Still imitating the old-timer's twanging accent he said, "I don't reckon there's any place like this here anywheres."

"For a spell?"

"For a spell . . ." he said, kissing her.

SPECIAL PREVIEW!

*If you like Westerns, here's a special look
at an exciting new novel*

CHEROKEE

The stunning story of family pride and frontier
justice by America's new star of the classic
Western, GILES TIPPETTE

The following is a preview of this new, action-packed
novel, available now from Jove Books . . . .

Howard said, "Son, I want you to get twenty-five thousand dollars in gold, get on your horse, and carry it up to a man in Oklahoma. I want you to give it to him and tell him who it's from, and tell him it's in repayment of the long-time debt I've had of him."

I didn't say anything for a moment. Instead I got up from the big double desk we were sitting at facing each other, and walked over to a little side table and poured us both out a little whiskey. I put water in Howard's. Out of the corner of my eye I could see him wince when I did it, but that was doctor's orders. I took the whiskey back over to the desk and handed Howard his tumbler. It was a little early in the afternoon for the drink but there wasn't much work to be done, it being the fall of the year.

Howard was father to me and my two brothers. Sometimes we called him Dad and sometimes Howard, and in years past quite a few other things. He liked for us to call him Howard because I think it made him feel younger and still a part of matters as pertained to our ranch and other businesses. Howard was in his mid-sixties, but it was a poor mid-sixties on account of a rifle bullet that had nicked his lungs some few years back and caused him breathing difficulties as well as some heart trouble. But even before that, some fifteen years previous, he had begun to go down after the death of our mother. It was not long after that he'd begun to train me to take his place and to run the ranch.

I was Justa Williams and, at the age of thirty-two, I was the boss of the Half-Moon ranch, the biggest along the Gulf Coast of Texas, and all its possessions. For all practical purposes I had been boss when Howard called me in one day and told me that he was turning the reins over to me, and that though he'd be on hand for advice should I want it, I was then and there the boss.

And now here he was asking me to take a large sum of money, company money, up to some party in Oklahoma. He could no more ask that of me than any of my two brothers or anybody else for that matter. Oh, he could ask, but he couldn't order. I held my whiskey glass out to his and we clinked rims, said "Luck," and then knocked them back as befits the toast. I wiped off my mouth and said, "Howard, I think you better tell me a little more about this. Twenty-five thousand dollars is a lot of money."

He looked down at his old gnarled hands for a moment and didn't say anything. I could tell it was one of his bad days and he was having trouble breathing. The whiskey helped a little, but he still looked like he ought to be in bed. He had a little bedroom right off the big office and sitting room we were in. There were plenty of big bedrooms in the big, old, rambling house that was the headquarters for the ranch, but he liked the little day room next to the office. He could lie in there when he didn't feel well enough to sit up and listen to me and my brothers talking about the ranch and such other business as came under discussion.

It hurt me to see him slumped down in his chair looking so old and frail and sunk into himself. I could remember him clearly when he was strong and hard-muscled and tall and straight. At six-foot I was a little taller than he'd been, but my 190 pounds were about the equal of his size when he'd been in health. It was from him that I'd inherited my big hands and arms and shoulders. My younger brother Ben, who was twenty-eight, was just about a copy of me except that he was a size smaller. Our middle brother, Norris, was the odd man out in the family. He was two years younger than me, but he was years and miles different from me and Ben and Howard in looks and build and general disposition toward life. Where we were dark he was fair; where we were hard he had a kind of soft look about him. Not that he was; to the contrary. Wasn't anything weak about Norris. He'd fight you at the tick of a clock. But he just didn't look that way. We all figured he'd taken after our mother, who was fair and yellow-haired and sort of delicate. And Norris was bookish like she had been. He'd gone through all the school that was available in our neck of the woods, and then he'd been sent up to the University at Austin. He handled all of our affairs outside of the ranch itself—but with my okay.

I said, "Dad, you are going to have to tell me what this money is to be used for. I've been running this ranch for a good many years and this is the first I've heard about any such debt. It seems to me you'd of mentioned a sum of that size before today."

He straightened up in his chair, and then heaved himself to his feet and walked the few steps to where his rocking chair was set near to the door of his bedroom. When he was settled he breathed heavy for a moment or two and then said, "Son, ain't there some way you can do this without me explaining? Just take my word for it that it needs doing and get it tended to?"

I got out a cigarillo, lit it, and studied Howard for a moment. He was dressed in an old shirt and a vest and a pair of jeans, but he had on his house slippers. That he'd gotten dressed up to talk to me was a sign that what he was talking about was important. When he was feeling fairly good he put on his boots, even though he wasn't going to take a step outside. Besides, he'd called me in in the middle of a workday, sent one of the hired hands out to fetch me in off the range. Usually, if he had something he wanted to talk about, he brought it up at the nightly meetings we always had after supper. I said, "Yes, Dad, if you want me to handle this matter without asking you any questions I can do that. But Ben and Norris are going to want to know why, especially Norris."

He put up a quick hand. "Oh, no, no. No. You can't tell them a thing about this. Don't even mention it to either one of them! God forbid."

I had to give a little laugh at that. Dad knew how our operation was run. I said, "Well, that might not be so easy, seeing as how Norris keeps the books. He might notice a sum like twenty-five thousand dollars just gone without any explanation."

He looked uncomfortable and fidgeted around in his rocking chair for a moment. "Son, you'll have to make up some story. I don't care what you do, but I don't want Ben or Norris knowing aught about this matter."

Well, he was starting to get my curiosity up. "Hell, Howard, what are you trying to hide? What's the big mystery here? How come *I* can know about the money but not my brothers?"

He looked down at his hands again, and I could see he felt miserable. "If I was up to it, *you* wouldn't even know." He kind of swept a hand over himself. "But you can see the shape I've come to. Pretty soon won't be enough left to bury the way I'm wasting away." He hesitated and looked away. It was clear he didn't want to talk about it. But he said, "Son, this is just something I got to get off my conscience before it comes my time. And I been feeling here lately that that time ain't far off. I done something pretty awful back a good number of years ago, and I just got to set it straight while I still got the time." He looked at me. "And you're my oldest son. You're the strong one in the family, the best of the litter. I ain't got nobody else I can trust to do this for me."

Well, there wasn't an awful lot I could say to that. Hell, if you came right down to it, it was still all Howard's money. Some years back he'd willed the three of us the ranch and all the Half-Moon holdings in a life will that gave us the property and its income even while he was still alive. But it was Howard who, forty years before, had come to the country as a young man and fought weather and bad luck and *bandidos* and Comanches and scalawags and carpetbaggers, and build this cattle and business empire that me and my brothers had been the beneficiaries of. True, we had each contributed our part to making the business better, but it had been Howard who had made it possible. So, it was still his money and he could do anything he wanted to with it. I told him as much.

He nodded. "I'm grateful to you, Justa. I know I'm asking considerable of you to ask you to undertake this errand for me without telling you the why and the whereofs of the matter, but it just ain't something I want you or yore brothers to know about."

I shrugged. I got a pencil and a piece of paper off my

desk. "Who is this party you want the money to go to? And what's his address?"

"Stevens. Charlie Stevens. And Justa, it ain't money, it's got to be gold."

I put down my pencil and stared at him. "What's the difference? Money is gold, gold is money. What the hell does it matter?"

"It matters," he said. He looked at the empty glass in his hand and then across at the whiskey. But he knew it was wishful thinking. Medically speaking, he wasn't supposed to have but one watered whiskey a day. Of course we all knew he snuck more than that when there was nobody around, but drinking alone gave him no pleasure. He said, "This is a matter that's got to be done a certain way. It's just the way and the rightness of the matter in my mind. I got to give the man back the money the same way I took it."

"But hell, Howard, gold is heavy. I bet twenty-five thousand dollars worth would weigh over fifty pounds. We'll have to ship it on the railroad, have it insured. Hell, we can just wire a bank draft."

He shook his head slowly. "Justa, you still don't understand the bones of the matter. You got to take the gold to Charlie on horseback. Just like I would if I could. You understand? I'm askin' you to stand in for me on this matter."

I threw my pencil down and stared at him. I nodded at the empty glass in his hand. "How many of them you snuck before you sent for me? You expect me to get on a horse and ride clear to Oklahoma carrying twenty-five thousand dollars in gold? And that without telling Norris or Ben a thing about it? Howard, are you getting senile? It's either that or you're drunk, and I'd rather you was drunk."

He nodded. "I don't blame you. It's just you don't understand the bones of this business. Justa, this is a weight I been carrying a good many years. I done the man wrong some time back, but it took a while for me to realize just how wrong I done him. When I could of set matters straight I was too young and too smug to think they needed setting a-right. Now that I can look back and be properly ashamed of what I done, it's too late for all of it. But I got to make what amends I can. If you knew the total of the whole business you'd agree with me that the matter has to be handled in just such a way."

I got up, got the whiskey bottle, and went over and poured him out about a half a tumblerful. It was dead against doctor's orders, but I could see he was in such misery, both in his heart and his body, that I figured the hell with what the doctor had to say. I went back over to my desk, poured myself out a pretty good slug, and then said, "All right, Howard, you want me to do something I find unreasonable. I think the least you can do is tell me something about what you call the 'bones' of the business."

"Justa, you done said you'd do it without asking me no questions."

"Well, goddam, Howard, that was when I thought you were just talking about the money. Now you're talking about me riding all the way clear up to goddam Oklahoma hauling a tow sack full of gold. Hell, Oklahoma is a pretty good little piece from here. Where in Oklahoma, by the way? What town?"

He shook his head. "I don't know," he said. "I've lost track of Charlie Stevens for better than twenty years."

"Aw, hell!" I said in disgust. I took a sip of my whiskey and got out another cigarillo and lit it, having let the first one go out unsmoked in the ashtray on my desk. We sat there in silence looking at each other. It was quiet in the house. The room we were sitting in had once been practically the whole house. It had been built out of big sawn timbers that Howard had had hauled in by ox teams after he'd started making some money. The rest of the house had just kind of grown as the need arose. Far off in the kitchen I could hear the sound of the two Mexican women going about the business of starting supper for the fourteen or fifteen hired hands and cowhands we kept about the place. A man named Tom Butterfield cooked for the family. Us boys had always called him Buttercup just to get him riled up. As near as I could figure he was as old as Howard and should have been in worse shape, judging by the amount of whiskey he could put away on a daily basis. Outside, in that year of 1896, it was a mild October and the rolling prairies of two-foot-high grass were curing off and turning a yellowish brown. We'd hay some of it, but the biggest part of it would be left standing to be grazed down by our cattle and horses. The Half-Moon was right on the Gulf Coast of Texas about ninety miles south of Houston. Our easternmost pastures led right up to the bay, where soft little waves came lapping in to water the salt grass and lay up a little beach of sand. All told we held better than sixty thousand deeded acres, but we grazed well over a quarter of a million. At any one time we ran from five thousand to ten thousand cattle, depending on the marketing season. A more gentle, healthy, temperate place to raise cattle could not be imagined. There was plenty of grass, plenty of water, and except for the heat of the summers, a climate that was kind to the development of beef.

The nearest town to us was Blessing. It was nearly seven miles away and we owned about half of it, including the bank, the hotel, the auction barn, and any number of town lots. Blessing had once been a railhead for the MKT railroad, but now it was a switching point between Laredo and San Antonio. It would have been no trouble at all to have shipped $25,000 to a bank or a business or some party in Oklahoma. But it sure as hell was a different proposition to ride a horse all that way and try to protect such a sum in gold. Hell, you'd need a packhorse just for the gold, let alone your own supplies. And such a ride would take at least three weeks, going hard, to get there, not counting coming back. And even if it was all right with Howard to come back on the train, that was another three days.

Of course that didn't count the time that would have to be spent looking for this Charlie Stevens. That is, if he wasn't dead. Hell, the whole idea was plain outlandish. But I didn't want to tell Howard that, not as serious as he seemed about it. But I said, "Howard, you know this is a busy time for us. We got to get the cattle in shape for winter, and then there's the haying. And there's also this business with the Jordans."

The Jordans were our nearest neighbors to the southwest. They were new to the country. They'd bought out the heirs of one of the earliest settlers in our part of the country. And now they were disputing our boundary line that was common with theirs. They'd brought in a surveyor who'd sent in a report that supported the Jordans' claim, so Norris had hired us a surveyor and he'd sent in a report that backed up *our* position. So now it looked like it was going to be work for the lawyers. And it was no small dispute. The Jordans were claiming almost nine thousand acres of our deeded land, and that was a considerable amount of grazing. But what was more worrisome, once that sort of action got started in an area it could spread like wildfire, and we'd spend half our time in court and hell only knows how much on lawyers just trying to hold on to what was ours. And the fact was that there was plenty of room for argument. Most land holdings in Matagorda County and other parts of the old Nueces Strip went back to Spanish land grants and grants from the Republic of Texas, and even some from when it first became a state. Such disputes were becoming common, and I wanted to put out our own little prairie fire before it got a good start and spread. Norris was mainly handling the matter, but it was important that I be on hand if some necessary decisions had to be made.

I finished my whiskey and got up. "Howard, I don't want to talk about this no more right now. You think on it overnight and we'll have a talk again tomorrow."

He said in a strong voice, "Justa, I know you think this is just the whim of a sick ol' man. That ain't the case. This is something that is mighty important to me. It's important to you and your brothers too. Ain't nobody in this family ever failed to pay off a debt. I ain't going to be the first one."

"Something I don't quite understand, Howard. You appear to be talking about some money you borrowed some twenty-five or thirty years ago. Is that right?"

"Maybe even a little longer than that."

"Howard, who the hell did you know had that kind of money that many years ago? Hell, you could have bought nearly all of Texas for that sum in them days."

He fiddled with his glass and then drank the last of his whiskey. He said, clearing his throat first, "Wasn't exactly twenty-five thousand. Was less. I'm kind of roughing in the interest."

"How much less was it? Still must have been a power of money. Interest is four percent right now, and I don't reckon it was anywhere near that high back then."

He looked uncomfortable. "Damnit, Justa, if I'd been lookin' for an argument I'd of sent for Norris! Now why don't you go on and do like I tell you and not jaw me to death about it!"

I give him a long look. "Who you trying to bully, old man? Now exactly how much was this original loan that you've 'roughed' in interest to bring it up to twenty-five thousand dollars?"

He looked at me defiantly for a moment, and then he said, "Five hunnert dollars."

I laughed a little. "Now that *is* roughing in a little interest," I said. "Five hundred to twenty-five *thousand*. How come you didn't pay this back twenty years ago when five hundred dollars wasn't more than a night of poker to you? And you and I both know you can't turn five hundred into twenty-five thousand in thirty years no matter how hard you try. Just exactly what kind of loan was this?"

He got slowly up out of his rocking chair, and then started shuffling the few steps toward his bedroom. At his door he turned and give me a hard look. "Wasn't no loan a'tall. I stole the money from the man. Now put an interest figure on that!"

I just stood there in amazement. Before I could speak he'd shut his door and disappeared from my view. "Hell!" I said. The idea of our daddy, Howard, stealing anything was just not a possibility I could reckon with. As far as I knew Howard had never owed anybody anything for any longer than it took to pay them back, and as for stealing, I'd known him to spend two days of his own time returning strayed cattle to his bitterest enemy. I could not conjure up a situation in which Howard would steal, and not only steal but let the crime go unredeemed for so long. Obviously he'd been a young man at the time, and he might have committed a breach of honesty as a callow youth, but there'd been plenty of years in between for him to have put the matter right rather than waiting until such a late date.

The truth be told, I didn't know whether to believe him or not. Howard's body might be failing him, but I'd never found cause to fault his mind. And yet they did say that when a man reached a certain age, his faculties seemed to go haywire and he got confused and went to making stuff up and forgetting everyday matters. But for the life of me, I just couldn't see that happening to Howard. And yet I couldn't believe he'd actually stolen $500 from a man and let it slide over all these years either.

I was about to leave the office when the bedroom door opened and Howard stood there. He said, "I charge you on your honor not to mention this to either of your brothers."

"Hell, Howard, I ain't going to mention it to nobody as far as that goes. But look here, let me ask you—"

I got no further. He had closed the door. I had seen the hurt and the helplessness in his face just before the door had closed. It did not make me feel very good. Now I was sorry I had questioned him so closely. But never in my wildest dreams would I have figured to stir up such a hornet's nest.

431